THE LONG DARK

Descent

Book: 1 of 3

Written by: B.J. Farmer

Edited by: Jeff Ford &
Kaz Morran: www.fiverr.com/kazmorran

Cover by: Alex Saskalidis@187Designz

Facebook: www.facebook.com/B.J.FarmerAuthor

Website: billyjoefarmer.com

Email: bill@billyjoefarmer.com

Dedicated to my love, Amanda.

D1528440

Table of Contents

Chapter 1

I vividly remember sitting at my tiny desk, in my tiny room, on the tiny, frigid island made of rock and gravel, scrutinizing the totality of my life choices. Cooped up on a five-acre island for twenty four hours of darkness every day, you tend to ruminate about such things. I kept telling myself, one more rotation and I'd never work another oil-drilling job again. I'd tell Miley to fuck off, and we'd go our separate ways. I'd take Avery with me, and we would find something else to do, even if it meant selling used cars in Pignuts, Arkansas. Couldn't be any worse than what we were already doing.

I should've told Miley no to begin with. If it weren't for my friends, I would have. Miley closed the drilling operation I ran in East Texas. It was the only job I'd stayed at long enough to get close to people, and, of course, it was on the list to be shit canned. Pretty fitting, I guess, considering most of my adult life followed the arc of Miley's whims and needs. He never much cared about my feelings—or anyone else's, for that matter. It was all about the money, baby.

I shook my head and sighed. I needed to stop thinking about things that depressed me, and I desperately needed to get some sleep before I started eating. When I was younger, I'd caroused with hookers, drank, took drugs, and did whatever the hell I wanted, no matter the harm to myself or others. But I'd grown up a lot during my time in East Texas. I'd started taking things seriously, and mostly gotten my mind right and my shit straight.

The loneliness and desolation I felt at the God-forsaken place people were calling the Patch reignited and reinvigorated my tendencies towards self-destructive behavior. Instead of paying dick goblins to cut lines of cocaine and rub their stinky titties in my face, I stayed in my room during my free time and ate myself into a stupor. That night, however, I chose to go to bed without gorging myself. Baby steps.

I made sure the alarms were set on both my watch and nightstand clock. At that point during the rotation, I was so worn out and depressed that one alarm just wouldn't cut it. I might not have been so exhausted had the emergency light not burned so damn red and bright, keeping me awake and pissed off a good part of the night.

Is it an emergency light if it shines all the time? It's more like a shine-until-there's-an-actual-emergency light; you know, just in case.

I asked Tom to take the bulb out, but he wouldn't because, he said, it was against OSHA regulations. I could deal with a minor safety violation, especially if it meant I'd get a decent night's sleep for once. I guessed the real reason Tom had refused was because he wanted to see my fat ass fall off the ladder trying to take the bulb out. I showed him. I never messed with it.

Red light be damned, I eventually drifted off to sleep. I'm not sure for how long—but at some point, I awoke to complete darkness. I wasn't sure if I was in the midst of a pleasant dream where the red light had been magically snuffed out by OSHA-hating pixies, or if I was awake and simply having the good fortune of the bulb having burned out. Either way, I was not sleeping, and it was out.

Not sure what time it was, I reached for my watch only to knock it to the floor. "Shit," I muttered as I nearly tumbled out of bed after it. Stumbling to my feet, I bent over where I thought it should've fallen only to misjudge my location and hit my head on the corner of the table. Reeling, I nearly tripped over my boots before finally catching my balance. I shook my head, trying to clear the light show taking place from all the stars I saw. I'd been knocked out several times in my life, but never by a table—not one thrown at me, anyway. I nearly marked that one off my bucket list.

Seriously, I thought. A warm trickle of blood flowed from a burgeoning knot above my right eye. I filled the room with a stream of curse words. After taking a few moments to clear my head and wipe the blood from my forehead and eye, I decided to try and find my flashlight before doing much more pitch-dark exploration.

I staggered through the darkness towards my desk, leaving a wake of destruction in my path. Anything that could be knocked over, spilled, or otherwise broken asunder was. After several minutes of probing the dark, cluttered recesses in and around my desk, I finally found what I was looking for. Click... Only, it didn't work.

I bashed the bastard, but pounding it on the desk wasn't nearly as effective as I'd hoped. The flashlight was dead. I'd just bought the damn thing the last time I was in Barrow, too. Cost me nearly fifty bucks. If Miley hadn't been such a tight ass, I wouldn't have needed to buy one for myself. I hoped Avery would have extra.

I blindly probed the floor until I found my watch. I was beginning to think the OSHA-hating pixies were responsible for more than the emergency light. I pushed buttons hard, fast, two at a time, and in every combination possible before concluding the damn thing had stopped working. My watch was dead, too.

Minutes later, and without breaking or lacerating any important body parts, I found my alarm clock. "Nothing fucking works," I growled as I tossed the clock across the room. Okay, I might've bashed it against the wall.

Aside from wondering what the hell was going on, I ran through my very small catalogue of things that might've caused everything to just die. As you should expect, I didn't have a clue. The only thing I could think of—and only because Avery had just brought it up a day earlier—was the issue of static electricity. I didn't know what the hell it was, but it sounded good at that moment.

It was time to find Avery. My speculating was getting me nowhere.

I stood in the center of the room, trying to get my bearings. It should've been much easier, especially given the cramped confines of my office/bedroom, but my head was still spinning from the trauma I'd received from the corner of the table. I needed my clothes. Despite being someone who had learned to be organized and always prepared for the work side of life, I never quite managed to transfer those positive qualities to my personal life. Lucky for me, I had slovenly shed my clothes near the door earlier that night.

I was putting on my second thermal shirt when something occurred to me. The used-to-be-menacing red emergency light was out. After all the sleepless nights, it stops working when I could've actually used it.

Within a few minutes, I was dressed and ready, minus one balaclava. I assumed Avery would get the power back up quickly. I would just find it when the lights got turned back on. Luckily, I had an old headlamp in the pocket of my parka, but, of course, the batteries were dead. The headlamp, I think, summed up life on the Patch accurately: something you think should be good, ends up being bad; or, at least not what you'd expected.

Though having only taken a couple steps outside, I was missing my balaclava. The wind pummeled my bare skin with wave after wave of frigid hitchhikers. I pulled the hell out of my hood strings until I looked like Kenny from South Park. A few steps later, I realized the only thing the taut hood did, besides make me look ridiculous, was put undesired pressure on my head wound. It sure as hell wasn't stopping the sleet from pelting my bare skin.

Being sleep-deprived as I was, I had a bit of a manic moment. I laughed as I remembered a conversation I'd had with Miley years earlier. It was before East Texas. It was even before I became drill superintendent. It was right before he'd sent his first exploratory crew to Barrow. He'd wanted me to go to the Arctic with one of the teams that had mapped promising drilling locations there. I had just done a winter rotation in North Dakota, so I told him I was sick of snow. He smiled at me and said, "Good. It doesn't snow that much above the Arctic Circle." I called bullshit on that, but he wouldn't yield, saying, "No, seriously, it's too cold and dry to snow in the winter months. I'm not fucking with you."

Luckily, he ended up needing me somewhere else, so I didn't go.

Hysterics aside, it is rare for it to snow above the Arctic Circle. Under normal conditions, it's just too cold and dry to get any significant precipitation. But that winter, it was warm—very warm. Now, when I say warm, I don't mean pull-out-your-tiniest-thong kind of warm. It's still cold as Titouan's icy heart, just not too cold to precipitate. Meteorologists marveled at how much snow had fallen and how much was still in the forecast

***

Titouan told Avery not to sleep at the COM shack. I didn't care where he slept, so I never made him sleep where he didn't want to. That, and he told me he hated sleeping there. He even said he would quit if I made him. When I asked him what the problem was, he said he didn't appreciate his bunkmate's propensity for farting. His exact words were, "A grown man's affinity for releasing gas should not extend to the subconsciousness of sleep. I should not have to pay for his nocturnal, gaseous incontinence."

I mean, how do you argue with that? Long story short, I knew to walk over to the COM shack rather than the nest where almost everyone else slept.

It was a brief walk over from my office, but the snowfall bizarrely worsened in those short two minutes. I could barely find the entrance; it was snowing so hard. The door (the one Avery felt the need to put a "Pull" sign on after Sam had pushed on it one too many times) was difficult to open because of the growing snowdrift in front of it. I cleared some of it away with my boot before trying to open the door again. Once I had cleared enough to get inside, I was greeted with several loud bangs.

"Who is there?" Avery asked, sounding like a kid whose nightlight had gone out.

"It's me."

"You scared me. I thought you were Titouan."

I laughed. "No, not Titouan. But he'll be here sooner than later; you can count on that."

Even though I knew Avery had battery-powered lanterns, the COM shack stayed pitch dark. I guess he'd been falling over crap looking for them, which leads us to the first thing you should know about Avery. Not only did he tend to be disheveled in appearance, he also tended to be equally disorganized. Titouan and I had told him to organize his workspace on numerous occasions. He'd obviously never got around to it.

"What the hell are you doing in here, besides clearly not keeping things organized?"

"Finally," he said. I heard a click, and then another one. Once he was sure the flashlight wouldn't turn on, he began to tap it with the palm of his hand. When that didn't bring about the desired effect, he slammed it against the table. He learned that from me.

"Chill, bud... come on."

Agitated, he said, "My flashlight always works."

Avery becomes attached to things. I guess that's maybe another thing you should know about him. His flashlight used to be black. But at this point, it'd been used so much, it was silver—or whatever the hell color aluminum is.

"Stop fixating on the damn thing. We're wasting time here. Time we don't have."

My words having—initially, at least—fallen on deaf ears, he flicked the switch several more times before finally giving up. He placed the flashlight gently on the table and began searching in earnest for alternative light sources.

Avery was a jack-of-all-trades guy when it came to electronics and communications. Since Miley ran a lean operation, Avery was a perfect fit, even though Miley himself would've most certainly disagreed. Actually, Miley thought he was an "overpaid geek". But Miley had a ridiculous aversion to anything or anyone he thought didn't add value to his business. He'd say, "If your hands aren't in the oil, all you're doing is costing me money. Not making it."

"We need to hurry, Avery," I reiterated.

"None of these are working."

"Change the batteries."

A few more bangs and a couple thuds later, a beam of light struck me in the face. "Jesus, Avery."

"Looks like you have some dried blood on your face. You will probably get an infection."

I waved him off. I had no intention of regaling him the great battle of the sharp corner.

Of the fifteen or so lanterns, headlamps, and flashlights he found, only six worked. We also found two large floodlights in the storage room that were connected to the COM Shack. Neither had bulbs. Avery said Tom had needed them for something, so he'd taken them. It was a moot point, really, as there was no electricity to power them. Still, Titouan was going to look at the totality of Avery's preparedness, and find it looking not so pretty.

Avery clucked his tongue several times before speaking. "Only one of our newer LED lamps works, and none of the flashlights. Whereas all of the older incandescent one's work. It is very strange, William. Very strange."

I grabbed one of the beaten-up flashlights and the batteries for my headlamp before saying, "Knowing Miley, he bought the cheapest shit he could find. We'll worry about this stuff later. We got to get to work, bud."

"I ordered the newer LED flashlights and lamps."

I knew he had. I had signed off on the requisitions. I was pretending he hadn't, I guess, to make him seem less incompetent. "We're making things worse by standing around."

He began to say something, but I quickly cut him off. He slung his work bag on his shoulder, grabbed as many of the working lamps as he could carry, and stomped off towards the exit.

With the night-shift people not having anything to do because of the power outage, they'd started milling around the Patch, trying to figure out what had happened. I heard a mixture of emotions coming from people. Some were happy as hell being out of work, while others were thinking about the end of rotation bonus and piling more blame onto Avery every second there was no production. I quickened my pace.

There are a couple other things you need to know about Avery. One, he's smart. He had a near-perfect score on his SAT. Where you come from, that might not be a big deal, but the area in Southern Indiana where we lived wasn't exactly known for coveting higher learning. The biggest academic pursuit was contemplating who would host the next mud bog.

Two, you've seen the prototypical nerd, right? The type with the pocket protector and trousers pulled up so high and tight it would take a Come Along and a front-end loader to de-wedge the bastards? Well, he's not exactly like that. He's more of a mismatched-sock, crazy-disheveled-hair, bad-at-social-cues, X-Files-shirt-wearing kind of nerd. Let's just say, he didn't always fit in with the people he worked with in the oil fields. If it weren't for me being in the leadership position I was in, I'm sure he'd have suffered his fair share of blackened eyes and bruises because of his social awkwardness.

It didn't take long for him to figure out something was wrong with the first generator. "Dang," he said. He opened the control box panel. "Shine the light here," he said, pointing a shadow-obscured finger where he needed the light.

Apparently, I was inept at shining a flashlight:

"Give it to me," he snapped.

Okay, there's one last thing you need to know about Avery. He was on his way to finding God by this point. Not your garden-variety, only-worship-on-Easter-and-Christmas finding God, have you. Not that easy. He found the Jehovah's Witness brand of God—or maybe they found him. Either way, as he'd said on numerous occasions, "Cussing was the antithesis of the exaltation of God." What's ironic about him finding God, though, was his startling lack of conversion where temper was concerned. Sam liked to rile Avery up by citing scripture that admonished his tantrums. Avery would try to ignore him, but I knew (and so did Sam) that it bothered him greatly.

Irritated because I hadn't given him the flashlight quickly enough, he snatched it from my hand. He circled the generator a couple times, pushing buttons inside the control panel, but nothing happened. Giving up on the first one, he moved to the second generator, where he went through the same routine with the same results. Aggravated, Avery slicked his mop of hair back with both hands and said, "I do not know how, but it appears to be more board failures."

I eyed him for a moment. He bounced his eyes back and forth between the two generators before beginning to snap his fingers. Not good. "Look, I'm going to go find Titouan and bring him back here, assuming he's not already on his way." Looking at him in a way I knew he would take seriously, I said, "If Titouan comes before I get back, you stall. Make up some shit. I don't care what. Just don't tell him the boards failed again."

He nodded. I began to walk away when he called out to me.

"William," he said. "Generator number one has a new board. Generator number three's board is a week and six days old. As prone to failure as these boards are, the current failure rate is outside the normal distribution by at least three deviations. These failures do not seem reasonable."

Avery had a very narrow band of emotions. The bookends of that spectrum were cruelty and indifference: he was quick to anger and slow to empathize. This made it difficult for people to relate to him, much less like him. Titouan's issues with Avery weren't based on Avery's lack of interpersonal communications and poor relationship-building skills. Titouan needed a patsy.

Avery didn't have the faculties of manipulation, dishonesty, and underhandedness to understand Titouan's real motives. He couldn't understand how Titouan wasn't so much impugning his ability to carry out his job, as he was using Avery's mostly-minor lapses to gloss over his own managerial misjudgments, while also staying in the good graces of Miley, who had already shared his displeasure about Avery. Win-win for Titouan.

Titouan tried to hide the production reports from me, but I had access to the network drive at corporate headquarters. I saw the downtime reports. Beginning the day after Titouan had culled several workers due to what he' claimed were productivity gains, there had been a marked increase in downtime at the Patch. In nearly every instance, Titouan attributed it to activities related directly to Avery and the maintenance department. Avery handled communications, networking, and most of the electrical work, including all power generation. At that point, I'd been relegated to running the maintenance department. Not only could Titouan knock off Avery, but he also had me in the mix. Again, win-win for Titouan.

"This simply is not possible. There has to be something else transpiring here." The look on his face as he said that, for the first time since his father had died, told me he was grappling with feelings he was ill-suited to handle. That worried me greatly.

"Come on, bud. You got this."

He nodded.

As I walked away, something Avery said struck me as odd. Careful to control my tone, especially given his frail mental condition, I asked, "You only mentioned two of the three generators. What's the matter with the third?"

He explained how we had three main generators, only two of which were needed at any given time. Generator number two wasn't working due to something unrelated to the control board. I guess I should've known that, but I'd grown detached and disinterested. That, and Titouan taking over my job as drill superintendent a few weeks into the rotation, had further sullied an already bad attitude towards all things oil drilling—all things Miley.

There were too many competing problems bouncing around in my head right now for me to fully register what he'd said. I left it at that.

"I'm not sure what's going on, Avery, but I know whatever it is, you can handle it. Don't beat yourself up." I gave a quick scan of the area, making sure the wrong ears wouldn't hear what I said. "Titouan's an asshole. He'll do everything in his power to put this on you. Don't give him any ammunition he doesn't already have." I waited to make sure he was paying attention to me. "Remember what I said. Not a word about them failing."

He nodded.

"I'll leave you to it. I'll make sure Titouan knows what's going on." I handed him my flashlight. "I'm pretty sure you'll need this more than me."

He began to speak but hesitated. Finally, he said, "I am going back to the COMs. I need a couple things. I am going to try another procedure to exhaust any potential diagnostic errors."

"Good idea." Anything to keep his mind occupied, I thought. "Maybe that'll work."

He snapped his fingers as he headed towards the COM Shack. Maybe not.

***

I heard, before seeing, someone approaching me. Before I could ask who he or she was, a harsh New England accent agitatedly asked, "What the hell is going on?"

"Glad to see you, too, Simon."

"Well, William?"

"Damn generators, again... but Avery's working on them as we speak."

"People are pissed, especially Harvey. He was watching porn on his tablet in the Commons again when the power went out. You should've heard him. He was cussing and pitching a damn fit about how Avery must've been doing an experiment or something that caused his tablet to stop working. Not that smart of a guy. Still, all kinds of strange things going on tonight, William."

Choosing to ignore the minefield that was Harvey and his porn problem, I said, "Yeah, I'm not sure what the hell's going on. Could be static electricity or something, you know?"

"Yeah..." He started to walk away but quickly turned back towards me and called out, "Hey, while I have you here—"

Simon was a bit of a talker. He was also one of the better riggers, so I usually bit hard on a tough stick and took his long-winded conversations like a man. I didn't have time that night. "I hate to be rude, Simon, but have you seen Sam or Jack?"

"Yeah, they're over at the dock drinking. Can't blame them with this shitty leadership," he said, his voice reeking of condescension.

"Thanks. I gotta run."

He kept talking with each step I took, until I eventually shouted, "Sorry—can't hear you over the wind."

"Jackass," he said.

By the time I got to the lean-to, it was snowing harder than I'd ever seen it snow at the Patch. It reminded me of my days staying with my aunt and uncle in Michigan. We would get these storms my uncle called "snow squalls". The snowfall was so thick you couldn't see more than an inch or two in front of you. That was awesome as a kid. It was a little different when you were older and had to work in it.

The door was locked. I began knocking, but it didn't take too many ticks before that knocking became a little more vigorous. "Come on in," called a man with a long, Eastern Kentucky drawl.

"I'd come on in if the damn door was unlocked," I said, as I kicked the hell out of it.

I heard someone struggling to unlock the door. I inhaled deeply as I waited. Finally, there was a tug at the door, but it didn't budge. "Oh, damn. Forgot 'bout the other latch."

The smell of kerosene and booze assaulted me as I entered. "Come on in and have a couple long pulls with us, William," Jack said, not a care in the world. Straight tequila will do that to you, and they were drinking it straight from a mostly-empty bottle.

"Yeah, someone has to work tonight. Apparently, you guys didn't get that memo," I told them.

"Hell, you got Faux Mulder and Emperor Tit. Not sure why you need us shit shovelers?" Sam said, laughing. The others joined in the chorus.

As much as I was aggravated with the nitwits, aside from Avery, the three idiots who were trying to drink the night away were most of the reason why I'd come to the Patch to begin with. They were all my good friends, which did make being their boss difficult.

I hovered my cold hands above the heater. "We might be down for a while... so we have to figure some stuff out."

Jack, who was by all appearances already drunk, asked, "What's going on?"

I gave him an exacerbated look. "Generators. You'd know that if you weren't in here."

"It bad?" Tom asked.

"Yeah, possibly really bad."

Jack looked at me and laughed. Well, he tried to stymie it, but wasn't able. Realizing the damage was already done, he went all in. "More time to drink."

Whether it was drugs, women, or insert-vice-here, he didn't have a stop button. I grabbed the bottle that was being grasped by both hands. "I'm serious, guys. Titouan is going to go apeshit if we don't get things figured out."

Tom stood up, elbowed Jack, adjusted his ball cap, and said, "What do you need us to do?"

We ran through our options. Since the generators were out, there was no heat. Even though it was relatively warm by Arctic standards, it was still very cold. The only space at the Patch large enough to accommodate everyone was the Commons. We decided the best option would be to round up what kerosene heaters we had and place them inside the Commons in case the power couldn't be brought up as quickly as we hoped. Cold people are angry people. I had one angry bastard to deal with, and that was enough for me. Speaking of which, it was time for me to pay the piper. I had to find Titouan.

Before I left, we quickly ran over the plans for a second time. Jack and Tom were going to help Avery. Sam was going to ready the Commons for the worst-case scenario, while also taking inventory on the things we would likely need in case of such an event. I was going to talk to Titouan. I got the shit end of the deal, by far.

***

It didn't take long to find him. He told me he'd circled the Patch a few times looking for me, and how he'd just come from the generators, but no one was there. He, of course, berated me because Avery wasn't working on them. I told him we must've left shortly before he'd gotten there. I also told him what I knew and exactly none of it pleased him. What infuriated him even more was when he saw Sam placing kerosene heaters inside the Commons. He asked me what was going on. I told him I was taking precautions in case the power couldn't be restored—it was mostly a precautionary thing.

"What the hell do you mean the power can't be restored? And you know you're not in charge here. Why are you making these calls behind my back?" he yelled.

I ground my teeth as I quickly formulated what not to say. "I said, in case. We have three generators not working right now, but that doesn't mean—"

"I guess Avery's blaming me?"

"He didn't say anything. Why would it be your fault?"

Ignoring my question, he said, "Avery isn't cut out for this, William. It's too much for him. I've known it the entire time."

Through gritted teeth, I said, "We've had one damn instance, besides today, when the power had completely gone out, and that was for, what, a half-hour or a little longer?"

"That's only the case because I've spent eighteen-thousand dollars on new controller boards for those generators. He repairs nothing. All he does is replace parts, and that's expensive. You know this."

"Look, Titouan, I trust Avery with this stuff. He knows a hell of a lot more about these things than either of us could dream of knowing. If he says something has to be replaced, I trust he knows what he's talking about. If anything, blame Miley for buying crappy generators."

"He doesn't know more than the makers of those so-called crappy generators. The engineer I talked to said the boards should be functioning perfectly well in the cold."

"Yeah, I'm sure he'd happily tell you how well they would operate in the Marianas Trench, too, if that's where you needed them."

Titouan angrily shook his head. "Let's just go to the generators. You can't separate your emotions where he is concerned."

One of these days, I thought. One of these fucking days. "Lead the way."

"Somebody has to, which is why I am, and you aren't."

Ten years prior, I would've punched him right in his pussy-ass little face. Instead, I forced a smile and said, "Yeah, sure."

He stomped off in the direction of the generators.

***

Essentially, things had gone from bad to worse. We found Avery well into the process of working on the generators. He had two control boxes completely taken apart, and Jack and Tom were nowhere to be seen. "Where's Jack and Tom, Avery?" I asked.

"Looking at the transformer," he mumbled, not bothering to look at either of us or translate the other bits of mumbleese.

"Why would they be looking at the transformer?" Titouan asked.

"Because I told them to."

"Is it too damn much to want a short update on what the hell is going on here?" Titouan continued.

Ignoring him, he focused on me. "Can you shine the flashlight into this box, William?"

I reluctantly grabbed the flashlight and shined it where he'd asked. He used what looked like a tiny pick to twice push a recessed yellow button. He went through the exact same process on the other board with exactly the same results. This time, however, after what he tried didn't bring about the desired result, he heaved the tiny pick, nearly falling to the ground for his effort.

After cursing under his breath and flailing angry hands in the air like a demented conductor, he blurted, "Just as I thought. Both boards are dead. We will be down until I can replace them."

"What the hell do you mean they're dead?" Titouan asked.

"I meant that colloquially. They are inanimate objects—"

"I know what the fuck you meant. Why would you need to change the boards? You changed one last week."

"I changed one last week because it stopped functioning correctly."

"That's six boards in eight weeks. Eighteen thousand dollars I've spent so far."

"We need two more."

Titouan paced. He started to say something but hesitated. He looked at me before settling his glare on Avery. "You fucking suck at your job. My ass is going to be in a sling because William coddles your ass—"

Sensing Titouan's rapidly increasing anger, I positioned myself between him and Avery. "Calm the fuck down. We'll change the boards, and when we're not half-frozen, we can talk about this."

Avery gave me this odd look, like I was late to the party and everyone else besides me knew the surprise. "We do not have backup boards."

Titouan shook but not from the cold. "Don't you put this on me, you weaselly fuck. This is you. This is your fault. There's a whole goddamn pile of them around here that you could use if you knew what the leaping-fuck you were doing."

I couldn't believe what I was hearing. "Wait... wait a minute. We don't have backup parts?"

They both answered no, but both had different arguments as to why there weren't replacements. Avery told Titouan he needed more boards because they were malfunctioning because of hot and cold cycling. He said something about the manufacturer using PCB boards that were too thin to function properly in the Arctic. Because of the nature of the control boxes, the internal temperature was either hot or cold, which caused the already too thin board to warp over time. It was this warping that caused the microcontrollers to unseat themselves from their sockets, resulting in the units' failures.

Titouan made the same argument he'd made to me a few minutes prior. The manufacturer said they should be working great. They shouldn't warp or do any of the things Avery complained about. After talking to the manufacture, Titouan refused to order more. He told Avery he'd better repair the boards, but Avery remained firm that what Titouan wanted was impossible.

"If you had hired someone who knew what they were doing instead of dragging along Gilbert Grape, here, we wouldn't be dealing with this."

When I left Avery the first time to look for Titouan, he was at a loss as to how to deal with the unfolding situation. After the brow beating Titouan had given him, that turmoil had evolved into unbridled anger. Knowing him as I did, I knew the next step in his evolutionary transformation would be rage with a chance of violence. Avery, even with his terrible temper, was generally non-confrontational. His many years of playground conditioning at the hands of bullies, jocks, and greater wimps had caused him to shy away from fighting. But there were limits, and Titouan was poking and prodding way past the boundary of those limits.

"Enough of the bullshit already. I don't care whose fault it is, because at this point, we're all fucked."

Titouan acted as if he were going to walk away, but instead of leaving, he started pacing again, back and forth, all the while muttering under his breath and working his hands in frantic motions. High-stress positions weren't in his wheelhouse.

The elephant in the room was evacuation. With the outfit I worked for, though, that would come with complications. Miley was not your typical business owner. He hadn't gotten rich by being a nice guy. If I were to tell you he crushed his competition, your natural proclivity might be to read that metaphorically. Don't make that mistake. He had a mob mentality of running a business, especially these days, in his later years.

Miley was making a hard push into the Arctic, and the word on the street was he was strapped for cash. Any downtime at the Patch, which by that time had become his biggest cash cow, would only exacerbate those cash-flow issues. With the potential of a month or longer of downtime because of the bad boards, it was unclear how Miley would react. I feared reprisals.

I was well on my way to being out the door before the power went out. I had jobs lined up for Avery and me back in Indiana. The reprisals and blacklisting wouldn't affect us, but they most certainly would my close friends. Tom and Sam had worked in the oil industry since Tom had graduated from high school. That's all they knew. Jack worked in some construction, but with the economy like it was, he'd be lucky to find much construction work.

As thoughts of reprisals poured through my mind, something odd occurred to me. Avery had told me how one of the generators was down because of bad bearings. Why hadn't he thought to check that generator's control board? Surely it was good, and if it were, why couldn't it be used in one of the ones with bad boards. We wouldn't be able to resume full operations with one operating generator, but we wouldn't have to evacuate, either. It would save a massive headache for everyone.

"Avery, you said one of the generators was on maintenance because of a bad bearing, right?"

"Yes." He turned to Titouan. "Bearings Titouan did not see fit to order."

Titouan stopped his pacing but didn't respond to Avery's barb.

As much as I was trying not to further stoke the dragon that was Avery, the pressure I felt finally let go in a torrent. "Well, take the damn board out of the one needing bearings, and put it in one of the two with bad boards. We should've already been doing this. Let's go!"

Titouan laughed, smacked himself in the face, and started rubbing his temples after the damage was done, talking to himself all the while.

"The safer choice would be to take the good bearings out of one of the generators with the bad board. The board is currently being held flat. There is a good chance once the screws are removed that the board might warp and become unusable."

"How long will that take?"

"Four to eight hours to take the bearings out."

"Versus taking just the board out?" Titouan asked.

"An hour and ten minutes," Avery said.

Titouan laughed again. "You make the fucking call, William. I'm not going to be responsible for his incompetence anymore. I refuse."

"You can't have it both ways. Either you're running the show, or you're not. If you are, then I suggest you do your job and tell us what to do."

"Fine. I'm telling you to make the call. You're fucking maintenance, aren't you?"

I exhaled deeply. "If I'm making the call, there's no need for you to stay here. All you're doing is making this harder."

"I'm not going anywhere, and you're going to make the damn call. This is your baby."

"You're something else, you..." I stopped myself from making things worse.

I counted to ten or a hundred before finally turning away from Titouan's sourpuss stare. "Take out the bearings and put them in the one with the working controller. Tom and Jack should be here any moment to help."

***

Titouan stood uncomfortably close to Avery while he worked. To Avery's credit, he was doing an amazing job of controlling himself. Titouan, on the other hand, was fit to be tied. Every passing second infuriated him a little more. So, when Avery stopped what he was doing with the bearings and moved to the control panel, Titouan erupted.

"What the fuck are you doing? The bearings aren't in the control box."

"It is too cold out here to take the bearings out only to find the control board is bad. I need to check this board before I go any farther," Avery said, continuing what he was doing.

I asked one more time for Titouan to leave. Much like Avery, he refused to make eye contact. His scowl was focused solely on Avery.

Avery ran through a procedure. He repeated it at least two time before sharing a glance with me. Damn, I thought. I didn't know how it was possible, but it sure seemed like things were getting worse.

"This board is bad, as well," Avery said, looking at me with wide eyes and shaking his head. "We are... we are down for the foreseeable future."

A whole lot worse.

There was a quick blur of motion. So, taken aback by current events, it didn't even register that Titouan had charged Avery until he was nearly on him. When I finally did get around to reacting, I slipped and fell to the ground, face planting into the quickly accumulating snow. Luckily Titouan slipped as well, allowing me time to regain my footing. I stretched out my left hand and got enough of his right ankle to make him fall to the ground.

"You're sabotaging this shit! Aren't you?" Titouan yelled as he floundered in the snow, slipping and falling at least two times before finally finding his footing.

By this point, I was back on my feet. Titouan bared his teeth as he shot his hands towards Avery's throat. I was able to grab hold of him just before he reached his target. Enraged at being held back, Titouan kicked, bit, and finally spit in Avery's direction. Apparently, it was an accurate shot as it hit Avery in the only uncovered part of his face besides his eyes: his mouth.

Avery wiped his mouth. His eyes grew large and angry. He belted a scream, which I hoped for a moment would reset his anger. It didn't. He pawed angrily at his mouth once more before charging. I turned Titouan away from Avery just in time for the screwdriver meant for him to find an alternate target. A pain shot through my shoulder, down my arm, and into my fingertips. He'd hit a nerve, but with my heavy parka, it didn't feel too deep or like it had done too much damage to my shoulder. Still, it stung like hell.

In one motion, I slung the bastard Titouan as far as I could throw him, grabbed Avery's hand, and slung him in the opposite direction. I then plucked the screwdriver from my shoulder and heaved it towards the Arctic Ocean.

I screamed out of anger and pain. "Stop it, you fucking idiots!" I was getting ready to tell Titouan exactly what I thought of him, when I heard someone yell, "What the hell is going on over there?"

"I'll tell you what's going on. Avery's crazy. He's sabotaging our equipment... trying to ruin my life!" Titouan yelled, his labored breaths forming ice clouds that obscured his crazed features.

"Shut up, Titouan. Now," I said, taking a step towards him just in case he refused.

Avery began to speak, but I told him to shut up, too.

Turning to Jack and Tom, I said, "I'm glad to see you guys."

Jack nodded; a big smile plastered on his face. Tom, on the other hand, looked on with pure disgust.

I explained what had happened, but I wasn't in the mood for many words. I asked Jack to take Avery back to the COM shack and stay there. Titouan and I were going to get a satellite phone, and we were going to call Miley. Finally, I told Tom to work with Sam on moving people to the Commons. The worst-case scenario was upon us.

As Jack guided Avery towards the COM Shack, I heard Avery say something under his breath. "Arnie was special needs. Not Gilbert Grape."

Fucking asshole, Titouan.

Chapter 2

"What do you mean yours doesn't work either? That's impossible."

"It means exactly what I said. It doesn't work." I held my satellite phone out and tried to power it on for him to see. This was after we both put in our spare batteries. "Did Avery sabotage these too?"

"Things don't happen just by chance, William."

"Look, scapegoating Avery isn't going to help you here. This is bigger than that."

"Why would I need to scapegoat him? He's just bad at his job."

"I've seen the damn reports you send to corporate. If you knew how to do your job, you'd have taken my credentials away when you took over."

Titouan's windburned face turned pallid. He began to speak, then stopped. I let him linger on his thoughts for a few ticks before retaking control of the conversation and redirecting it in what I hoped would be a more productive direction. What we were dealing with was much bigger than falsified reports and fragile egos. We were dealing with a real emergency, where real people could freeze to death if we didn't act appropriately. I hated the idea of it, but I needed Titouan to come on board, be on the same page as me. Fighting only wasted time. Time, we didn't have.

"Besides these phones, did he sabotage my watch... my alarm clock? Maybe it's sheer coincidence, but Simon told me Harvey's tablet died when the power went out—"

"Your watch?"

"And the alarm clock and everything else. All dead." I picked up my watch off the table and tossed it to him. I then pulled the power plug out of the wall, walked over to my desk, grabbed a new battery out of its package, and inserted it into the clock. I then tried to give it to Titouan for his inspection.
He tossed my watch back but refused to take the clock. Apparently, he had gotten the point.

Titouan had a seat at my desk. The lamp cast a wicked shadow across his face. He sat there seemingly deep in thought, possibly collecting his next wave of irrational thoughts and readying for the next tirade that would make him forget how he wouldn't be able to scapegoat his way through this.

Then something unexpected happened. He rubbed his bare wrist and said, "My watch stopped working too. That's why I didn't wear it."

"Avery's my best friend, but I assure you, if you had evidence in place of irrational hatred, I could easily be swayed away from defending him. But that really doesn't matter, and neither does the fact that you didn't order replacement boards. It doesn't matter. We're past that. Right now, we can only take care of the only variable that matters. Our people. Either of us getting fired or barred from the industry won't mean shit if someone freezes to death. You can find another damn line of work. If someone dies, well, we'll be making license plates in prison."

He walked over to the window. There was nothing to see outside aside from snow and darkness, but that didn't stop him from looking. "I don't know what to do, William."

That was the first sign of unfettered weakness I'd ever seen from him. There is such a thing as a leader who is hard, demanding, and difficult to please but who still manages to be civil and decent. Titouan was rarely either. He represented everything people hated about their bosses. He was smug, arrogant; and, worse—entitled. He got into Wharton because his dad signed some checks. He'd taken my job at the Patch weeks after graduating from Wharton because his dad was friends with Miley, and because he was the largest shareholder besides Miley.

Titouan thought he'd promenade into the Patch as he did everywhere else, and his dad's power, money, and influence would allow him to do as little or as much as he wanted and succeed no matter which option he chose. He was surprised when that didn't pan out. People like Titouan blame other people when things don't go as planned. People like those who worked at the Patch didn't give a rat's ass about people who blame other people for their own problems. My main role at that point was playing arbiter between the two disparate worlds.

I wanted to hope that maybe he was coming to his senses. I saw a twenty-five-year-old kid with barely any experience asking, even if it weren't outright, for help. I could let him drown because of his prior transgressions and, potentially, for causing needless pain for my friends and coworkers; or, I could help him swim and cause them as little pain as possible. I chose to help him. It certainly wasn't because I had suddenly become deluded enough to think he'd had a moment of life-altering clarity. I didn't buy that for a second. Momentarily humbled was much more likely. I helped him because of the very reason I was there in the first place, and that was only because of my friends. Otherwise, I couldn't have cared less if he floundered until he drowned in his own wretched bile.

I told him to go to the Commons and make sure people were as comfortable as possible. I also told him to omit the part, unless asked, about the satellite phones not working. Was that the right thing to do? Probably not, but then, there didn't seem to be an easy or obvious ways of handling crap like this. I was flying by the seat of my pants.

Stone-faced and pale, Titouan shook his head and left without saying another word.

I decided to check the screwdriver wound before talking to Avery. I pulled my parka off, peeled off the thermal shirts I had on underneath, and saw, to my surprise, that Avery had inflicted a gnarly wound on my shoulder. I probably needed a couple stitches but decided that was too much of a luxury then and now. I couldn't find any Band-Aids, alcohol, or anything I might've used to clean or dress the wound. I ended up using a makeshift bandage fashioned from a strip of cloth torn off a shirt I found lying on the floor. Sanitary? Probably not. It would absorb the blood, though. That was good enough for me.

I got dressed and grabbed the phones. I hoped Avery could make up for stabbing me by fixing one of them. The way things were going, I had my doubts.

***

I noticed someone standing outside the COM shack. The visibility was so poor I couldn't see who it was until I got within a few feet.

"What are you doing out here, Jack?" I asked.

"I had to step out a couple minutes. I think Avery was getting ready to, uh, talk to me about Jehovah."

"Never a bad time for the Lord," I said, patting him on the arm. "Let's go in. I'll bring up my shoulder. That'll take his mind off proselytizing."

Jack didn't laugh. "I need to talk to you."

Jack was a chill California guy, or at least that's what he would say about himself. He didn't normally get excited about much of anything. Usually, that was the result of being on too many drugs, but he appeared, at that moment, to be sober, which was a bit odd. Just an hour earlier, he was well on his way to being shitfaced. "What's up?"

He proceeded to tell me that when he and Tom were checking the transformer, they had heard things: "Something weird off in the distance. The wind was blowing so hard, it was difficult to make out what it was."

"You don't know what you heard?" I asked.

"Look, William... I know I've been drinking. I know you know this. But I heard footsteps. I tried to tell Tom, but you know how he gets when he's working on something. He tunes everything out. That, and he drank more than I had."

That got an eye raise from me. Jack normally outdrank everyone. "Go on."

"I tried to concentrate on what we were doing, but I kept hearing shit over and over again. It was snowing so hard, and I couldn't see three feet in front of me. It sobered me up real quick, bro."

"You got drunk and heard noises in the dark? That's what you're freaked out about?"

"Yeah." He shook his head and smirked before continuing, "Tom gave me the same crap... until he heard it himself. He stopped cold what he was doing. The bastard asked me if I'd heard it, too. I'm like, no shit, dude. Whatever it was, was snorting and sniffing its ass off out there on the ice. To make things worse, he wanted to go check and see what it was."

"Well?"

"We walked for several minutes but didn't see or hear a damn thing after that. We were getting ready to turn around when a truck rumbled to life a good distance from where we were. That was followed by— and I shit you not—what sounded like hundreds of feet pounding on the ice."

Knowing Tom and, especially, Jack, as I did, part of me thought it was the booze talking. But aside from that, I had too much on my mind to get bogged down by snorts and trucks on the ice. "That's a lot to take in—"

"What if the generators being dead are connected somehow to what we heard?"

"Sabotage?"

"Maybe. That would explain a lot, wouldn't it?"

"I'm pretty sure the only sabotage that happened here was perpetrated by the company who makes and sells those janky pieces-of-crap control boards in those generators."

I could tell by the look on his face he thought I wasn't taking him seriously.

"You know there shouldn't be anything out on that ice like that, especially a big-ass truck that clearly wasn't on the ice road. You don't do that, bro, unless you're trying to do some underhanded shit."

I shrugged. "I don't know. I'm sorry... I just don't know."

He searched my face for any signs of how I was processing the information he'd given me. The problem was, I wasn't processing it. My mind at that point was about as faulty as the generators. It was on overload. There comes a point during a crisis when—and I don't give a crap who you are—you don't have anything in your knowledge bank telling you what to do as the next wave of chaos washes over you. It becomes a pileup of unprocessed clutter in your mind. All I wanted to do was get warm, take a load off, and forget about everything for a little while.

"Come on, Jack. Let's go in. I'm about frozen to death. You can't be too far behind." My hand was on the door handle when I turned to him. "Hang with me, man. I don't mean to blow you off. I'm trying to do the best I can."

He wasn't exactly encouraged by my less than enthusiastic support but nodded in agreement, nonetheless.

***

I handed the phones to Avery. "You mind looking at these?"

He nodded, unaffected by being given two more faulty pieces of electronic equipment.

He started taking one of them apart. Not bothering to look up at me, he asked, "Are you okay?"

That got Jack's attention. A wicked grin stretched across his mug as I said, "I'll be okay.... Stab Titouan next time, instead of me."

Avery cocked his head to the side and said, "Okay."

Jack wheeled an office chair next to the heater and motioned for me to have a seat. I thanked him. I took off my mitts and tossed them on the floor next to the heater. God, that heat felt good. Jack leaned up against the wall and slid to a seated position on the floor. He looked like shit.

I soon fell into a trance, listening to Avery check over the phones and watching the dancing flames emanating from the kerosene heater. When Avery began to speak, I was startled into a semi-alertness.

"There are multiple resister and IC failures in the circuitry of both phones."

"IC?" I asked.

"Simplified, an IC is a processor or microchip."

I didn't have to know what either one of those things was to know it was a bad deal. The important part of what he'd said was that this represented one more piece of the puzzle laid upon the table. I wasn't smart enough to put it together, but I hoped Avery was. "None of this makes any sense," I said.

Jack was sleeping or passed out by that point, or at least his loud snoring indicated he was.

"The commonality here is everything I have checked, including the boards in the generators, have bad ICs. These failures being the result of some random event, is simply implausible, at best. Something other than a random event had to have caused what is happening here."

Avery viewed the doodads on the table. The look on his face evolved from one of confusion and concern to one bordering on mirth, as a thin smile materialized on his normally stolid mug. Making sure I was watching, he waved his hands over the phones and electronic thingamajigs scattered across the large desk. I wasn't sure what point he was trying to make other than assuming none of it worked—I already knew that. I waited patiently for him to make his point.

A wave of irritation washed over his face as he repeated the exaggerated movement with his hand. "Well?" He finally asked.

"Well, what?"

He waved for the third time—

"Will you please get on with it?"

"All of this is Fluke."

"What—huh? I thought you said this couldn't be a random event."

"You do not get it?"

I sighed. "No... I really don't."

"My voltmeter and oscilloscope are both manufactured by Fluke. It was a play on words." His smile faded. Replaced by his normal look of indifference.

Sometimes, Avery would take a step out of his self-defined world of rules and predictability to take a stab at being funny. He had a difficult time understanding Sam, but there was something about him that Avery occasionally tried to mimic, at least on some basic level. He almost always failed miserably, but he tried. Normally, I would at least try to laugh, but this time I didn't have any patience.

I rolled my eyes. "Fucking really? Nerd jokes at a time like this. You realize Titouan wouldn't care if you were tied up and thrown into the Chukchi Sea."

"That was bad. Even for you, dude," Jack said, seemingly jolted out of his booze-induced catatonic state.

"It is frozen," Avery said.

"Huh?" Jack said, confused.

"The Chukchi Sea is frozen."

"I know it's frozen," I said, frustrated but still amused because of the expression on Jack's face.

Changing the subject, I asked, "I take it you have a theory on what's happening?"

Showing no expression that would lead anyone to believe he was upset about being rebuked for his lousy joke, he tapped semi-rhythmically on the table with his knuckles. That was always a sure sign of him being nervous about something. He would wiggle a leg, tap on things with his fingers or knuckles, make different noises with his mouth, and a multitude of other ticks. Whatever it was he was thinking, he didn't want to share. He began to say something but stopped. Instead, he went about tapping at the desk again, looking back and forth between me and Jack.

I waited for Avery to gather his thoughts, which ended up being a couple long minutes. "Before I delve too deeply, I want to also mention something worth noting." He pointed to several flashlights and headlamps on the table. "This pile here works." He pointed to another pile. "These do not."

Jack was getting impatient. "You think you can just cut to the chase?"

Avery went back to tapping. Jack was making him nervous. "Most of the ones still working are of the incandescent variety. I have one working LED flashlight. The others are non-functional. Just as with my test equipment, if it has ICs, then it probably does not work."

I'd like to think I'm a decently smart guy, but I didn't understand what Avery was getting at. I guess he assumed everyone knew as much as he did and would instantly get the connection he was trying to make. The problem was, we didn't. All I heard was gibberish. "Just tell me what all of this means."

"I was not finished, William. The difference between the older incandescent and the newer LED lights is the incandescent lights do not have the sensitive components that LED lights have."

I shook my head. I still didn't know what he was talking about.

Jack was up on his feet and putting on his gloves. "Men, I think I'm going to go check on things at the Commons, throw up, and take a piss, but not necessarily in that order."

"Jack, it wouldn't hurt to have the Polar Bear gun around just in case," I said.

"Will do," he said, nodding, before leaving.

Jack's departure seemed to alleviate some of Avery's anxiety. "Do you know what they call me here?"

I hesitated. "Well, I know some of the names—"

"The nickname."

My first instinct was to think about the baby seal I saw being eaten the first day I stepped foot on the Patch. Even as stressed out as I was, thinking about Sam talk about "Ol' Faux Mulder" made me laugh nearly every time he said it. "Yeah, I'm not completely sure, bud."

"They call me Faux Mulder, but you are aware of that."

"Well, I knew something about you and the X-Files, but I never heard you being called that."

He knew most people working on the Patch wouldn't be receptive to some of the ideas he had about things—or at least I thought he knew. But at the beginning of the rotation, Avery would sit in the Commons and talk about his theories on aliens and who-knows-what-else. By about day three, a few guys had started making fun of him. After that, he spent most of his time alone in the COM shack.

"One scenario..." He paused several more seconds, contemplating his next words, before rapidly saying, "An EMP attack is the only scenario I can think of that could do the damage we are seeing. I have racked my brain trying to come up with an alternative, but I simply cannot. Everything leads to this conclusion."

"A what?"

"I knew you would react this way," he said, rolling his eyes and flailing his arms towards the sky like a thirteen-year-old girl who had her cell phone taken away. "I suppose you think I am crazy like everybody else does."

"I'm not making fun of you, Avery. I frankly don't know what the fuck you're talking about."

He couldn't believe I didn't know what an EMP was. The fact of the matter was, I didn't. I mean, I had heard of it, yes, but I'd also heard of nuclear fission, but I sure as hell didn't know how to explain it, nor did I even casually understand it.

"You do not know?"

Exacerbated, I said, "No. I honestly don't."

Shaking his head in disbelief, he said, "EMP stands for Electromagnetic Pulse. It can be man-made or natural. Lightning, for example, is a form of an EMP. An example of a man-made EMP would be a high-altitude nuclear explosion—"

I stopped him. I tried hard not to shake my head in disgust but failed miserably. "Not been too many lighting strikes here at the Patch lately. That only leaves the other option, right?"

"Can you think of any alternatives?"

"Not at the moment. But I'm just as inclined to believe snow pixies sabotaged our generators because global warming was melting their snow pixie homes as I am of someone nuking us. Besides, even if your theory was reasonable, and I can't see how it is, we would've heard it or seen it." I paused. I told myself not to say it, but I had too much bundled up frustration not to. "This is just more conspiracy shit. That's all this is."

Unaffected, he continued, "Depending on the altitude of the detonation, we might not have heard it. Besides, the Northern Lights have been extra vivid lately, which could be a telltale sign of magnetic field perturbation. When the U.S. government detonated Starfish Prime in 1969, the effect from gamma and X-rays, when interacting and perturbing the Earth's magnetic field, produced, to observers on the ground, an effect that looked almost exactly like the Northern Lights. I am not crazy, William. There is evidence here to justify my hypothesis."

Thinking about what he'd said made my eyes glaze over. "I know you believe your... hypothesis. Just like Fox Mulder believed aliens were real. I think you are rationalizing here. This isn't the X-Files."

"Well, if you are using the X-Files to prove your point, you realize aliens were proven to be real during the series. Fox ended up being vindicated. Besides, I am clearly able, much to your and everyone else's chagrin, to separate reality from fiction. I am dead serious."

I had to get away from him before I said something I would regret. I breathed deeply before saying, "I'll take everything you said into consideration. I need to go talk to everyone, and I'm pretty sure I can't tell them we've been nuked."

Avery was like a dam getting ready to explode. He needed to bleed off some of the pressure. "It would not have to be a nuclear blast. An EMP attack could be a ground-based attack. The United States military has working EMP weapons."

I picked up my by-then toasty mitts off the floor. I zipped and buttoned up my parka. I walked to the door and started to pull on the handle when I looked back at Avery and said, "If what you say is true, why are our batteries still working? I don't want to hear about any of the other shit. Answer that specific question."

I got the you're-a-dumbass stink-eye for that one. Another thing I guess I should've known. "An EMP would not destroy our batteries. In fact, an EMP should have the effect of charging our batteries."

I pulled my hood over my head. "Okay. I gotta go."

"William," Avery said, losing the stink-eye, "if this was an EMP attack, it had to be in close proximity to damage the phones and smaller electronics."

I thought about asking him to explain why the attack had to be so close but chose not to because of the potential colloquy I'd have to endure. Instead, I nodded, took a breath, and told Avery to meet at the Commons in thirty minutes.

The wind and snow were ferocious. I nearly dropped my lamp during a particularly strong gust. Visibility was as low as my spirits. The look on Avery's face as he made his case didn't bolster my emotional state. Normally, conspiracy-type things filled him with delight, but he wasn't happy. Hell, he was frightened, and that in of itself was scary to me.

The idea of getting nuked seemed to have, for me, at least, gone the way of the old USSR and the might and resolve it once had. But then I guessed that was an outmoded way of thinking. There were many other countries that had nuclear technology, and a fair amount of them weren't exactly our friends. Still, I couldn't make myself believe the EMP nonsense. Even as I shook my head in disgust about what I was actually having to think about, the ringing alarm-bells going off in my consciousness, tolling the oddity of our current events, let me know I shouldn't wall off the EMP hypothesis, especially if more evidence presented itself.

***

"I was told you would be in here. Why aren't you over at the Commons with everyone else, Sam?"

He pulled at one side of his handlebar mustache before saying, "Son, 'ere is some pissed off and scared people over 'ere. 'At and it's too damn crowded for my likin, 'specially with your boy, Tit, over 'ere. I got 'is here heater. I'll be just fine."

I exhaled a giant gulp of air. The cloud of frozen particulates clearly showed it was too cold in what essentially was an enclosed, thinly insulated lean-to to be comfortable, and probably too cold to be safe, for that matter.

He ignored my show. "Why would they be scared? Not exactly the first time the power has been down."

"You don't reckon 'ese people ain't got electric watches and tablets? Surely ya don't thank we as dumb as ol' Tit does, do ya? With 'em all dyin' at once, and everybody talkin 'bout it, ya lucky people ain't beatin on ol' Faux's door over 'ere lookin for answers."

"Yeah, there are a few things down... It's probably just static electricity or something like that, and you know I don't think like Titouan does. I love you dickheads. Besides, if I were like Titouan, I would've asked you what the hell an electric watch was."

I'd heard Avery talking about static electricity causing issues with working on electronics, especially in the Arctic. He'd said it was something about how cold and dry the air was. I knew Sam probably wouldn't buy it, but I honestly didn't know what else to say. The truth was off-limits, because I wasn't even sure at that point what the actual truth was. I knew, on the one hand, about the failure of the generators and almost all our electronics for no good reason. On the other hand, there was the EMP option. I decided to not concentrate on the potential causes because I didn't want to go crazy. Instead, I focused on the main event: we were screwed.

Sam gave me exactly the look I'd expected from him. The look of him knowing damn well I was full of shit. We went all the way back to my first weeks in Texas after leaving Indiana. I was pretty much penniless and living in a single-room dive when we met. You know, the kind of dive you pay by the week and one where you share a bathroom with however many other people live there. Anyway, Sam had lived there too. He'd started working for Miley Construction Company two days before I had. Yes, the same Miley who owns the Patch—the one-percenters own all kinds of shit. The point being, he knew me from way back.

"You don't have a clue 'bout what the fuck you just said, do you? You probably heard Faux talkin 'bout it."

"Yeah, I gotta say, it did sound better when he said it."

Sam moved his chair closer to the heater before saying, "Since we done 'liminated static electricity, what else does 'at leave?"

Sam had a knack of wading through the bullshit. "We're not exactly sure. Avery does have at least one theory about what possibly could've happened."

"Yeah, what might 'at be? Little gray men turn our lights out—dittle our buttholes when we was sleepin?"

"Only your butthole," I said.

"Seriously, what does Avery thank? I gotta know, son."

I sighed. "He thinks someone exploded a nuke in space and that was supposed to have caused our stuff to go tits up."

Sam stared at the floor for a few moments shaking his head. Through a single open eye and with a cocked head and a shit-eating grin, he said, "I guess the nuke created the static 'lectricity you was talkin 'bout too?"

It wasn't so much that I believed what Avery had said. It was more about feeling inadequate and helpless about not knowing what else to believe. We were helpless in the damn middle of the Arctic, for Christ's sake. Yes, I was at the mercy of a highly flawed theory, but I knew my own limits. The fact of the matter was, and this still sounds ridiculous, I couldn't come up with a better explanation for what had happened. Shit normally doesn't stop working like we saw during that period. I didn't reply because I didn't know anything that would satisfy him. Maybe I shrugged. I don't remember.

"Holy hell and nervous Mother Mary. You don't buy 'at shit, do ya?"

"Honestly, I don't know what the hell to buy or believe at this point."

I was more than ready to change the subject. A dark mood was sweeping over me, and I needed to get a grip on it. I needed to keep moving. I couldn't sit there and dwell on things that were simply out of my control. I had to concentrate on those things I could, and hope Titouan wouldn't try to get in my way as I trudged through them.

"The reason I came over here, besides being worried about you being in here, is I need to know when the next supply truck is due?"

I could tell he wasn't ready to leave the conversation, but he acquiesced. He wheeled his chair back over to his desk and shuffled through some paperwork. "Looks like next Wednesday."

"Five damn days, Sam? You have to be kidding me."

"Son, thangs are fixin ta get whole lot worse. Are you sure you can't get 'em generators runnin?"

"I assume you're going to give me more bad news?"

"'Member when you asked me ta check on the kerosene? Well, I did. We might have 'nough for a couple days if we stretch the hell out of it. Maybe. None of 'em stooges at corporate imagined us ever needin ta heat 'is place with just kerosene."

"We should've stayed in East Texas."

He nodded in agreement and then asked, "What's the plan?"

"Round up all the kerosene you have and put it under lock and key. I'll put Jack in charge of making sure it's used most efficiently. Then bring this heater over to the Commons. You don't know it yet, but you have to come to Barrow with me."

"I got yer back, son."

"If that's the case, you want to go over to the Commons and tell everybody how screwed they are?"

He patted me on the back. "Nah, but if 'ey start beatin on you, I'll call the police."

"I feel better already."

Chapter 3

The structure of authority is durable when things go as planned. Add some chaos into the situation and see how quickly power erodes. After a few months of me working construction, Miley must've seen something in me. That, or I was the only sucker who would do it. He made me his closer. When the performance of an operation was below Miley's high expectations, I would go in and try to meet them. If I couldn't, we closed it down and let everyone go. I'm not especially proud of those days, but if I'm to glean something positive from them, it would be the insight I gained.

In almost every instance, employees assumed I was there to close the operation, and no matter how much I explained how that was the last resort, they didn't buy it. Everyone hated me because I was the big, mean closer, and they sure as hell weren't going to put forth any more effort than they had to. That would make my job too easy, and, most importantly, they would gain nothing from it. They would take long breaks, slack off instead of working, and essentially lie down. Hell, some of them would go ahead and quit, leaving me with empty positions I couldn't fill, because no one wanted to board an already sinking ship. It was a self-fulfilling prophecy of sorts.

When I got to the Commons, Titouan was locked outside. He was getting a small taste of what I went through, and I wasn't in the same league of asshole as he was. Everyone was already upset that I'd been demoted. Those most displeased by this turn of events were the loyal, senior workers who worked with me in East Texas. Couple that anger they had from his unexpected ascension with supply shortages, horrible work environment, and, at that point, a complete power outage, and what you had was a bonafide shitty situation for everyone involved.

You're probably thinking, well, if they were loyal to you, then it makes sense they would treat Titouan like dirt. I was their friend, no doubt about that. Most of them had a family and kids, though. They wouldn't give up their paychecks out of loyalty to me, and I wouldn't have wanted them to. Loyalty wasn't the problem.

The issues were driven almost exclusively because of Titouan. He was one of the most arrogant people I had ever known, and there were a lot of dickheads in the oil business. Imagine, if you will, listening to a person who is at least fifteen years your junior, who never worked a day in his life before coming to work at the Patch, drone on about "the ethics of work". He liked to give speeches before, during, and after he bitched you out. Besides hearing himself talk, he loved to talk about his ancestry. "Charles de Gaulle is my fourth cousin," he would say. The first time de Gaulle got namedropped, Sam was unsure why he should care. "Who the hell's 'at sonofabitch? Is he French? No wonder Tit's such a dick." Long story short, Titouan was his own worst enemy and should've never been running an operation as big as the Patch.

"Fuck you and fuck them, William. They all hate me, and it's all your fault."

"I'm not sure that's an accurate appraisal, but if it makes you feel better, run with it. Don't let reality spoil it for you."

"I wouldn't have hired any of those Cretans from East Texas. They're your people. Not mine."

He was deluded. All I wanted to do was go into the Commons and explain to people what I believed needed to be done. I didn't want to litigate things with him again. I told him on numerous occasions how he had to make relationships with his (not my) employees, and I wouldn't stand in his way or make things difficult for him. It was his job to make or break things, and, well, he broke the hell out of them.

Titouan was hilariously fuming by that point. Almost to the level of six-year-old-didn't-get-his-toy-at-Wal-Mart fuming. I thought he'd stomp his feet at any moment, so I gloriously waited him out. I wanted to hear the unadulterated, unfiltered reason why he was standing outside. It almost made the power being out worth it.

He finally couldn't hold it in any longer. "I let them know even though the power was out, there were things that needed to be done. They didn't like what I said, so they threatened to kick my ass if I didn't leave."

"You really think now is the best time for all of that?"

"They don't have anything better to do."

A sardonic laugh quietly escaped my lips before I could stop it. I quickly covered it up with a derisive sigh, which wasn't much better, but I doubt he noticed. "Here's the deal. I'm going to go tell everyone what's going on, and you're going to stand beside me and smile, but you aren't going to say a damn word. You fucked that up. I won't let you make things worse than they already are because you have a gigantic chip on your shoulder. Got it?"

He didn't say a word to me. He gave me this weird shake of the head. It wasn't an okay-I-got-it head shake. It was a big, fat I-hate-your-fucking-guts-palsy of a head shake, but to his credit, he at least didn't argue with me.

The Commons had a gray haze and an acrid smell to it. There were too many kerosene heaters in too small of a space, but even then, it was not comfortably warm. For whatever reason, the Commons had the thinnest walls of any living space on the patch. Most of the other buildings, especially the bunkrooms, had walls bordering on a foot thick. The walls in the Commons were less by a quarter inch or so. Compounding things, it had two large windows. It was the best we could do, given all the shittier options.

Titouan and I weaved through elbows and knees on our way to the front of the room. I heard some grumbling because of Titouan's re-entrance, but no one did anything stupid. Not all the complaints were Titouan-related. People were frustrated and cold, and if they were anything like I was, they were also getting hungry. With no way to cook food, it was only going to get worse. I was hoping I could give a pep talk, but it became pretty clear that nothing I could say, barring flipping a switch to turn the power back on, would make people feel better, so I decided to be honest and direct. I needed to be the one doing the talking. No Titouan allowed.

I turned to face him and said, "Remember, stay quiet. I'll handle this."

Titouan's eyes said what his mouth didn't: fuck you.

I was relieved when I saw Avery walk in, more so that Jack was with him. He'd shut him down if he started talking too much. The last thing we needed was Avery crying nuke-attack while I was trying to calm people. I started thinking about the double whammy of Titouan insulting people in the front of the room, and Avery nuke-talking in the back. As cold as it was, I was sweating.

For every face I could see, I knew there were two times as many I couldn't. But the ones I could see didn't look happy. By simple extrapolation, I knew that added up to a bunch of unhappy people. Considering they were sitting in a room lit by a just a few lamps and heated by fewer heaters, and breathing in air freshened with ass and kerosene—not to mention being stranded in one of the most inhospitable places on the planet, without electricity, running water, the ability to cook food; and having all their electric devices fail at the same time—who could blame them? I sure as hell couldn't. Titouan—as I think everyone should know by this point, but sometimes you have to emphasize and reemphasize the bad bits to make sure it was crystal clear—wasn't exactly the cherry on top.

The one wild card was how long it would take Miley to find out that contact was lost with the Patch. He was a micromanager to be sure, but he also had to have his long weekends for hunting. Some people called Miley's headquarters in Barrow "Little Africa", because it had so many stuffed animals from the African continent. That time of the year, he was gone most weekends on some safari or hunting expedition in some far-flung place we plebes couldn't even imagine affording. Even if he wouldn't find out for a couple days, those two days would be longer than I was willing to wait for help. We were going as soon as possible.

Speaking loudly enough so people in the back could hear me, while also trying not to yell at those in the front, I said, "I've decided that I, along with a few other people, are going to Barrow for help. There is nothing we can do to get the power back up, and every communication device I'm aware of is down. If anyone has a working satellite phone, please speak now." I paused for a moment, but there was only silence. I continued. "Jack is going to stay and make sure everyone is as comfortable as possible. He's in charge. Any questions?"

There was a smattering of questions, most of which were impossible to answer because we simply didn't know. One person asked about how healthy it was for them to breathe all the smoke and gasses coming from the kerosene heaters. I didn't know the answer, but if I had to guess, I'd say it wasn't. I ho-hummed around how it wouldn't hurt them if they didn't have to breathe it very long. Another person asked if it could've been corporate sabotage. I was honestly a bit flabbergasted by that one. Maybe Jack was right, but even if that were the case, it didn't explain why everything failed at once.

One man furiously asked what would cause his laptop and watch to die at the same time. Apparently, he was using his tablet when it died for no reason—this wasn't the guy watching porn, for the sake of accuracy. There was a chorus of people yelling similar questions. I told them the honest truth. We didn't know. I made sure to tell them my personal stuff was damaged too. I'm not sure why, but them knowing I was affected, too, seemed to have a calming effect on some of the angrier ones.

I wasn't used to dealing with angry employees. Most of these people were my good friends, but even friends weren't immune to being cold, irritated, and afraid. It was a bad deal, but I tried to be as calm and level-headed as possible.

After the last question was asked, I walked back through the crowd and talked to several people one on one. I felt the hot stare of Titouan behind me. That told me I needed to move him to the back of the room and away from people as quickly as possible. He was going with us to Barrow. It was obvious he couldn't be allowed to stay at the Patch while I was gone.

Along with Titouan, I decided Sam and Tom would be good to have in case of emergencies. They both were good mechanics, and we'd almost surely need them, assuming we could get the Shining started. Avery would have to come so he could explain the technical details of what had happened. Hopefully, I could get him to omit some of the fruity details. Tish would round out the rest of the crew. While she wasn't technically a nurse yet, she was interning with our RN. I figured it wouldn't hurt to have her along in case something happened on the way, and it helped she knew Barrow better than any of the rest of us put together.

In a perfect world, I would've hopped in a vehicle and quickly driven the ten miles via ice road to Barrow for help—or better: everyone could've jumped into a bus and ridden to Barrow and then to a nice, warm hotel room. Between our location and Miley's penchant for complete control, those two options didn't exist anywhere except my wildest fantasies.

We had two vehicles at the Patch. One was a front loader that was used to clear the Patch of snow and for other utility work. The other vehicle was a modified 1978 or 1979 Snow-Trac. It had been modified so many times over the years that it was hard to tell. It could've been older or newer by several years. I knew it was there because I saw it every time I went to check inventories with Sam at the lean-to.

All other departures from the Patch were controlled by headquarters in Barrow. The only way someone could depart the Patch was on leave time, in an emergency, or if Miley wanting to see you. Those were the only options. Everyone who signed up to work on the Patch knew what they were getting into, but they were paid handsomely in return. One perk was the pay. It was, arguably, the only perk.

It was time to tell Titouan the good news. That I was making the decisions at that point, and he was around, literally, for the ride. I asked him to follow me to the supply room, which was about the only place in the Commons where I could talk to him one on one. If all went well, I wouldn't have to punch him the face.

I didn't waste any time. "You're coming with us to Barrow."

"I take it that you're forcing me to go, then?"

"Miley has shit on these people, and, since you run this place, you are an extension of Miley. This power outage was the last straw. People hated you before, and now, well, it's just not safe for you here, anymore. Think of it as a favor."

"Doing me a favor, my ass. You're going to lead me around like a little puppy until we get to Barrow. Then you can wave hello to Miley and be out the door, leaving me to take responsibility for this disaster. While Avery might not have sabotaged things, I still believe his incompetence caused the issues here. So, this disaster is on him. Not me. Bravo, though, I'm sure you'll get your job back. Great play, William."

"Did you order the parts Avery asked for, yes or no?"

"No."

"Why?"

"Because we had already spent too much money. That's why. And the damn engineer told me the boards should be good... I told you this already."

"Horseshit. In no universe do you shut down a multimillion-dollar-a-week plant over a part that costs a couple grand. If they taught you that at Wharton, they need to give Daddy Warbucks his money back."

"Fuck you, William."

I shrugged. "It is what it is, right, Titouan?"

"What if I decide not to go?"

"You'll probably get your ass beaten to within inches of your life. Good enough reason?"

"You aren't my boss."

"No. I'm not, but I'm acting in your best interest, whether you like it or not. Besides, no one is going to listen to you until this is all sorted out, and then they still probably won't. We're at fucking critical mass here. You sticking around will only cause the meltdown. Grow up and accept things as they are."

"I'll fire them if they don't listen."

"That's your fucking takeaway—seriously? Our people are trapped on this cube of gravel, stuck in a cold room filled with noxious gas, with no running water, and no warm food to eat. Are you so damn obtuse and stubborn that you think they care about being fired? Hell, if that meant them getting a quick ride out of here, I bet almost every damn one of them would take that deal. Shit, sign me up. I'll go with 'em."

"Go to hell."

"Tell you what, go in there and tell them they're fired. I'll go with you. Let's go." He didn't move.

I made sure my lamp was turned up bright enough that he could see my face before saying, "You're a grown man. I won't make you go, but I'll be damned if I'll be responsible for you. If you stay, you're on your own. Got it?"

"Whatever."

He slammed the door in my face as he left the supply room. It'd only been a matter of time before I lost it with him. He was an idiot man-child. There was part of me that didn't care if he went or not. Maybe he needed an ass-beating to set him straight.

I saw Jack, Sam, and Avery waiting near the exit. Just the people I needed to see.

"Titouan took outta here pretty quick. He looked like he had a turd cocked sideways, or you done took away his training wheels, one," Sam said.

Avery raised his hand like he wasn't sure about something Sam had said. I playfully slapped his arm down. He looked at me like he wasn't joking.

"Jack, if you don't mind, I'd like you to stay here and take care of everyone. Try to make sure they're as comfortable as possible, without burning the damn place down or suffocating them. Do me a square, and open the Commons' doors occasionally, to let some fresh air in."

Jack smiled and nodded. "Sucks I'm going to miss that ride over, but I get what you're saying about the air. Smells like feet and ass in here."

"Speaking of making it to Barrow, Jack and Avery, I need one of you to round up Tom, preferably Jack. And get to work on the Shining. Make it as ready as you can."

"I'll get the gun and a few other thangs, then I'll head on over," Sam said.

I nodded at him.

"You realize it will not start, correct?" Avery interrupted. "Because it is a diesel, a cold engine cylinder will transfer most of the heat created during compression, via the second law of thermodynamics, and—"

Interrupting Avery's physics lesson before it really got going but realizing Avery was right about it not starting, I said, "Didn't think about the small detail of warming the damn block. How in the hell are we going to do that?"

"We've got a forced-air heater that I use to keep the water tanks thawed. We could use that to warm it, I think. It gobbles the kerosene, but we shouldn't need it that long," Jack said.

Avery combed his wild hair with his fingers before saying, "The heater will not work because it needs electricity for ignition."

"There's a battery in the front loader. You should be able to use that as your power source, assuming you know how to convert the twenty-four-volt battery down to the needed voltage of the heater," Jack said, happy with himself. "You're not the only smart one here."

Avery clucked his tongue and gave Jack a sour look. "Easy."

"Good. Let's do it," Jack said, slapping him on the back.

***

They called it the Shining because, well, it looked sort of like the tracked vehicle in one short shot at the beginning of the movie—not the actual vehicle that the mom and son escaped in at the end. No one for sure could remember who'd first started calling it that, but it stuck. It's odd that the vehicle was named after a scary movie, because even as scary as The Shining was, the idea of driving its namesake ten-plus miles in horrible conditions was even scarier, especially since no one had ever seen it run.

I had just come from asking Tish to come along with us. I had hoped to hear the diesel engine as I neared the lean-to. No dice. Instead, I saw Avery's over-exaggerated hand movements, followed by Jack shouting at him. "Just wire it up. It doesn't have to be perfect, dammit."

"If I do this incorrectly, we destroy the battery. We do not have another," Avery said. The electric lamp jutting out from under his hood made him look like a hairy cyborg or something.

"Stop being a drama queen, Avery," Tom said. He had exactly no patience for Avery.

I distanced myself from the fight. I didn't want to fuel the fire.

"There," Avery said. The heater came to life.

"I told you that would work, Avery," Jack said, not smiling. "You're stubborn as shit. You know that."

Ignoring Jack, Avery said, "Whoever wired this engine did a horrendous job."

"Well, we don't have time to fix it, so don't touch it," Tom said, fearing Avery's OCD would compel him to fix what he thought was done poorly.

"When was the last time this was actually driven? —started, for that matter?" Jack asked.

Everyone looked at one another, hoping someone would say yesterday or two weeks ago or even a couple months ago, but no one knew.

"Not very confidence-inspiring, is it?" Jack said.

I laughed. "Freeze here, or freeze stranded on the ice. Either way, you're frozen."

"Very poetic, William. I wish Sam was here to regale us with some of his stuff. You know, like the dick-slapper poem? Remember that one?" Jack said, letting go of a hardy laugh.

"Yeah, I remember. He had a bit too much to drink that night..."

"Sam is a Neanderthal," Avery said.

"He hears you say that, he'll give you the ol' dick-slapper," Jack said, now chortling.

Avery rolled his eyes.

"Alright, let's fire this thing up," I said, looking at Jack and shaking my head. Dick-slapper.

The good news was the battery in the Shining was charged; it turned over. The bad news was it didn't start. We waited a few minutes and tried it again. Still nothing. Avery decided the heater needed to be closer to the engine block. I feared that it would melt the rubber tracks, but it really didn't matter if they were melted or not if it wouldn't start.

Thirty minutes or so passed before we tried starting it again. It turned over, but nothing happened. The fear was the battery would die. Because of the conditions on the patch, any battery installed outside was supposed to be checked every two weeks. Being that the Shining tended to be forgotten, its preventative maintenance might've gotten skipped. Compounding that issue was that the guy who changed the batteries tended to be, well, damn lazy.

"Can I offer a suggestion?" Avery asked.

Everyone sighed in unison. Tom finally broke the silence. "As long as you can say it in under a minute."

Tom stole my line.

"I will just show you rather than tell you, then."

"Dammit, Avery," Tom said. I grabbed his arm and motioned for him to let him do it. Tom clenched his fist and jaws. He cursed loudly but conceded that Avery might've been their best chance at getting it started.

Avery proceeded to climb into the engine box of the Shining. I couldn't exactly see what he was doing because Avery's lamp hid his hands from view. All I could do at that point was hope he knew what he was doing. Part of me wanted to grab him out of there, but the other part that had seen him do wicked-clever things in the past won out. Tom chimed in a few times but decided to save his sanity by walking far enough away that he couldn't see inside the engine bay.

Avery finished whatever it was he did and hurriedly put his mittens back on. With a wry smile, he said, "Try it now."

Jack climbed onto the tracks and then into the driver's seat. I jumped onto the tracks and around to the engine bay. I took one of my gloves off and gave the engine block a feel. It was warm to the touch at that point. I gave Jack the thumbs up. Time seemed to slow down for those few moments. He cranked it a couple times before it knocked and sputtered for a few seconds before dying. On the next try, however, with a huge plume of black smoke belching from the exhaust, it came to life.

Avery walked to the driver's side and smugly said, "I told you that would work." He was extremely proud of himself, not to mention remembering how smug Jack was with him about the heater. He was less willing to run the victory lap around Tom. Good thing. Sam told me later that Tom had been the one who wired it up incorrectly. The important part was it was running. Now, we just had to hope the damn thing would continue running for the ten or so miles to Barrow.

Chapter 4

We had spent a great deal of time making the Shining operational. It was out of the lean-to, and Tom was driving it around the small open area in the center of the Patch. The positives were that it was still running and seemed to operate more or less as it was supposed to. The negatives, well—it was the Shining, and no one knew if it would run for ten minutes or ten hours. We would hope for the best but expect the worst.

We were nearly finished putting the few items we decided to take with us in the back when Titouan showed up. He didn't say a word to anyone. Instead, he climbed the passenger-side track, put his bag on the rear bench seat, and sat beside it. His pouty face and bag in the seat told everyone he didn't want a traveling companion. As if anyone was going to cry because he hogged the seat. By that point, he would've had to pay someone to sit by him.

Everyone was loaded in and as ready as you would expect, given the circumstances. Tom was tasked with driving, well, because he just was. None of us had ever driven on the ice road before, so it didn't matter who drove. I mean, it wasn't rocket science. If we looked for blowouts, which were essentially holes in the ice, and kept our speed under seven miles an hour, we wouldn't fall through the ice and drown in the cold waters of the Arctic Ocean. No pressure.

It didn't take long for the first issue to arise. We knew we had to stay near or below seven miles per hour. The problem was the damn speedometer stopped working a few minutes into the trip. It's not like the Shining was a hot rod or anything near that because it sputtered along to beat all hell. It was disconcerting not being able to see if we were going a safe speed.

Avery, of course, chimed in, saying, "Because we are not near land, rebounding pressure waves should not be an issue. If we stay in nominal proximity to the desired speed, we should not fall through the ice."

I think he was talking about the cause of blowouts, but who knows. No clarification was asked for.

The second and more serious issue was the recent heavy snow covering the ice road. There's a good deal of maintenance that goes into keeping an ice road safe. I didn't know everything there was to know about it, or even a little bit, but I knew that unmaintained ice was bad, and that we had ten or so miles of it to navigate.

Thanks to the unprecedented amount of snow the Patch and outlying areas had received, Tom thought he could feel when the Shining went too far off course to the left or right because of the banks of plowed snow on either side. Since they were steep and of a decent size, we hoped they would corral us on the ice road, like how go-cart tracks keep go-karts from leaving the course.

We were maybe fifteen minutes into our trip when Avery spoke up. "Has anyone thought about what it might feel like to drown?"

"Sweet Jesus," Tish said, surprise raising the pitch of her voice an octave or two. "Really?"

"It is a serious question," Avery said, without a hint of inflection that would lead us to believe he was joking. "It is times like this when we should contemplate living and all the travails that coincide with it," he continued.

"Tell your idiot to shut up, William," Titouan cried from the back seat.

"Oh, hell, ya guys are bein too rough on ol' boy. He just breakin the ice," Sam said.

"You're as bad as he is. Except you realize what you're doing," Tish said.

Sam feigned being offended.

A few moments passed, and Avery was back at it. "I am genuinely curious—"

"It's been warm lately... You realize we could fall through the ice at any point," Titouan said. He sighed and then paused before finishing his thought. "The only thing you're worse at than fixing things is conversation."

"Even with the warmer-than-average temperatures, the ice is thick enough to support the weight of this vehicle. We are safe, Titouan," Avery said. "Besides, fear should motivate us to explore the unknown, find out about it, and see if that fear is warranted. If I am analyzing what you just said, I think your fear is based on false conclusions derived from ignorance."

Titouan began saying something shitty when I interrupted him. "Well, I'm pretty sure fear of falling through the ice is warranted. How about you ease up a bit? I didn't bring my antacids."

"It's pretty damn obvious nobody wants ta talk about yer serious question, Faux. I'll talk 'bout somethin 'at scared me ta death when I's a youngin. It ain't 'bout fallin through no damn ice, 'cause I don't swim, and the cold makes my pecker shrivel up, but it's still a story 'bout 'plorin fear. Like you done said, it's important ta explore yer fears."

"Oh, God," Tom said, sighing.

"I swear on my Aunt Betsy's life, God rest her soul, what I'm 'bout ta say is true. It all started when I's in the Ozarks with my friends." He stopped. "Can ya hear me back 'ere, Titouan?"

"Eat shit," Titouan barked.

I turned to Sam and said, "Just get it over with."

He cleared his throat before continuing. "I was prolly 'bout fifteen at the time, I'd guess. Anyways, we lost track of time doing what boys do, and it was nightfall 'fore we knew it. I got separated from 'em on the way home and got plum turned around. As I's tryin ta find my way back home, I wandered on 'is huge glowin light. It was one of 'em orb saucer thangs."

There was barely enough light in the cab for me to see the look on Tom's face. From what I could see, it was priceless. It was somewhere between wanting to laugh hysterically and longing for a deep plunge to the bottom of the Chukchi Sea to make it all stop. I personally knew it was going to be a bullshit story, because Sam grew up in Eastern Kentucky, and as poor as they were, I doubted he traveled with his friends to the Ozarks or much anywhere outside the holler. That, and, it was Sam, and that was pretty much all that needed to be said.

"I stopped in my tracks, my butthole puckered so tight I could've done squeezed coal into a diamond," he continued, "nearly fallin ta the ground, I struggled for my balance. The glowin light was on me 'fore I could run away. The next thang I knowed I was in 'is big vat of green slime, strugglin ta breath and fightin for my life. I felt like I was gonna die. Then, as I was takin my last breath, this short, big-eyed little alien fella waddled in the room, with his short legs and whatnot, and pushed some buttons on a panel thingamajiggy. I was out like a light. When I woke up the next mornin... I's so happy ta be alive. That is, until I felt 'is horrible pain in my backside. My butthole hurt somethin awful... the damn aliens must've gave me a back-side burner... Ya know, shoed the ol' brown mare... I could understand if 'ey wanted to check my eyesight or somethin... but why my butthole? I reckon I'm an alien abductor or whatnot."

If I'm completely honest, I couldn't help but laughing. It was kind of what we all needed, even though, as expected, Titouan wasn't happy. He made some, let's just say, stereotypical and geographically-insensitive slurs towards Sam and a certain sister of his. Sam was probably pissed off, but played things as usual, saying, "What, you jealous 'cause it wasn't you gettin the diddlin, Tit? I know all 'bout you fancy-pants, boys."

Avery, on the other hand, was seemingly unaffected. No harm, no foul, right?

"There are cases I have read about where abductees had similar experiences. Of course, those experiences were articulated better and much less crudely than your silly recitation, but they are documented, nonetheless. But you know what, I get that you are making fun of me," Avery said, more let down about the episode not being real than he was mad about Sam making fun of him. "Furthermore, it is alien abductee—"

A panicked cry came from the back seat. Titouan had screeched something that barley resembled speech. I flicked on my headlamp and quickly scanned the cab before asking what the hell was going on.

"Outside... I saw something," he said, this time mostly comprehensible.

I turned my headlamp off and scanned what little real-estate I could see outside the Shining. I couldn't see anything that would elicit Titouan's outburst. I turned back towards him. "What the hell is going on?"

Titouan sat slumped over in his seat, seemingly so he couldn't look out the window, or so someone couldn't look in. I wasn't sure. "I don't know," he said, his eyes still wide with fear.

"What the hell do you mean, you don't know?"

I turned towards Tish. She shook her head, letting me know she didn't see anything. I then glanced at Avery. His face told a different story. "What did you see, bud?"

He didn't reply.

"Someone tell me what the hell is going on," I said, losing my temper.

"I'm not sure, William," Titouan, said, now calmer, but with a tremble in his voice. "It was a man... I think. He looked different. Like he was sick, maybe."

"You'ins is a bunch of loons," Sam said. I told him to be quiet.

Avery finally spoke up. "I am not sure what it was. When I heard Titouan yell, I turned to look at him but saw something moving out of my right periphery. I am not sure what it was, or if it was anything. I did not, however, see a person."

"Stop the truck, Tom," I said.

"What the hell are you doing, William? Don't stop. You're not understanding me. He didn't look right."

"Tell me what the hell was wrong with him. We can't just leave him out there if he's sick," I said.

Titouan paused before speaking. "His eyes looked weird. I don't know, William. He just didn't look normal, that's all."

"You think the sonofabitch would look like Cindy Crawford? He's out in 'is damn blizzard," Sam said.

"Fuck you," Titouan said.

"I was just makin my story up, Tit. You don't have to try to one-up me with your—"

"Stop it, Sam. No time for this."

"Just givin him some of his own medicine."

"Please, Sam."

He grumbled something under his breath.

I thought I'd ask the sanest person in the cab what he saw. "Tom?"

"Nothing. I don't think we should stop, though."

"Let's just get to Barrow," Tish said.

I sighed. "Just stop. Maybe he's our help, and he broke down."

Tom shook his head but abided. The Shining's diesel engine sputtered and knocked, nearly dying before coming to a full stop.

"I'm thinkin if he was help, I'm doubtin he'd come alone, fellas. Somethin's not right 'bout 'is," Sam said, finally getting the potential seriousness of the situation.

"Let's fucking go, okay," Titouan yelled. "If he's been out in this, he's probably near death, anyway."

I hesitated for a few moments, thinking about what the hell I should do before finally saying, "I'm going to check outside. We can't leave whoever it is out here to die."

"You're crazy," Titouan said.

I took a step down onto the track. "I'll be a minute. That's all."

Tish joined Titouan in her desire for me to not go outside. "There are polar bears out there. This is stupid. Please, let's just go. Besides, Titouan is probably just trying to get back at us for making him come."

"Fuck you. I know what I fucking saw, okay?"

"You're an asshole, you know that?" Tish yelled over her shoulder.

"Just shut up, you two. I'll take the gun." And use it on myself, I thought.

"It's a bad idea," she continued.

As I closed the door, I heard Tom telling Tish everything was going to be all right. If anyone could make her feel better, it would be Tom. They'd become almost inseparable since she'd come to the Patch. Of course, working around the kind of people who worked at the Patch, rumors were flying about them being more than just friends. I never asked. If Tom had wanted me to know, he would've told me. I do know they took leave together on at least two occasions. I heard they were going hunting together. Like I said, I didn't ask. I approved their leaves.

I walked around to the rear of the Shining. I opened the rear hatch and grabbed the rifle we kept for protection from polar bears wondering onto the Patch looking for scraps. I had no clue what kind of gun it was. I just knew it had a scope that didn't work. The glass had a nasty crack running down the center, and you could barely see through it. "Just aim down the side of the barrel," Sam told me. "You ain't goin ta hit nothin, anyways." I rotated my injured shoulder. That wasn't going to make things any easier if I had to fire the rifle. Thanks, Avery.

I walked back to the front of the Shining and told Tom to throw the truck in reverse and follow close behind me just in case shit went down. He yelled out a string of expletives I barely heard over the grinding gears. He apparently couldn't get it to go in reverse. He wanted to turn around and follow me, but I told him not to. "Keep the piece of crap pointed towards Barrow... and be ready to roll if something happens."

"Yeah, we'll book it out of here," Tom said.

Smartass.

I adjusted my headlamp and began walking in the direction we'd come. I didn't see anything, but I swore to God I heard something. The farther I got away from the Shining, the less I could hear the rumble of the diesel, and the more attuned I became with my surroundings. There was a flurry of what sounded like snorts very close to where I was standing. I'd taken the polar bear educational experience given by one of our safety trainers; I didn't remember polar bears making sounds like the ones I was hearing. The sniffing noise sounded like what children make when they've cried too much. There was a convulsion and then a gasp for air. If it was a polar bear, the bastard was sick.

I have no remnant of pride to lie and say I wasn't scared, because I was. There was a large part of my copious self who wanted to take off and run towards the Shining. The faint knocking of the diesel engine and the comfort of knowing it was still within running distance kept me sane enough to keep walking away from it, as weird as that sounds. It wasn't, however, enough to make me yell out to whoever (or whatever) might be out there, which is what I should've done but couldn't. I was well past the outer limits of my gallantry. It was time for me to go. If it were someone who was supposed to check on us, the bastard should've followed us, or yelled or something, instead of doing nothing. I wasn't about to try to track him down, and I didn't think it was my job to do so. I honored what I considered my duty to check on him. I didn't see him. I was finished.

I backed away slowly at first. My senses were in overload. I heard everything but probably nothing. Still, I had an ominous feeling that someone or something was near, maybe even stalking me. Humans have goosebumps for a reason. The vestiges of our primal past were in full effect all up and down my arms, nape of my neck, and legs. Adrenaline coursed through my body, and I was in unadulterated fight-or-flight mode. Since I didn't have anything obvious to fight, and because it wouldn't have mattered at that point even if I had, I chose flight—big time. I was running back to the Shining before I even realized it.

I tried to jump on the tracks but missed and knocked the holy hell out of my shin as a result. I dropped my rifle in the snow, and my headlamp now covered my eyes. "Fuck," I screamed out in both pain and fear. I was overcome. I felt a hand pulling at my parka, but I didn't scream... outwardly, anyway. Inside, my neurotransmitters were all up in a tizzy, slinging dopamine like a meth dealer in a trailer park. I turned my head to see who or what had a grip on me. My head spun, but my hood didn't. All I ended up seeing was its furry lining and the plastic backing of my lamp. I was trapped in the moment; in a prison created by my own fear. I was flailing my arms like I imagined Titouan did when he didn't get his thirty presents for Arbor Day.

"William, what in the hell is a matter with you? Get a grip, son," Sam said, firmly but not angrily.

I flipped away my hood, turning my head and hoping I didn't imagine the comforting twang of Sam's voice. It was him. If I hadn't been so overcome, I would've been embarrassed. Tom, now out of the cab with the rifle in his hands, stood watch for my self-imagined foe. Seeing him with the gun helped me regain some of my senses. I got up, dusted myself off, and climbed into the cab of the Shining. My heartbeat was beginning to slow, but my stomach was in knots, not to mention the horrible ache I felt in my shin. I thought I might throw up or pass out or, more likely, both.

"What the hell happened back there, William?" Tom asked as he shut the driver's door.

"I'm tellin you all, everybody done went crazy," Sam said, as he entered the Shining.

"I'm not sure. Could have been a polar bear... or nothing. I'm not sure," I said, still panting. "I think we should get going, though."

Tom waited for Sam to get situated between Avery and Tish before taking off.

If it hadn't been for the sound of the engine and the clunk of the rubber treads on the snow, you could've heard a pin drop in the cab for at least the next thirty or so uneventful minutes. Under different circumstances, I would've received serious grief over how I'd handled myself during the search for Titouan's ghost. Everyone was so lost in their own contemplation that my faux pas didn't even register.

I noticed Tom looking at me. "What?"

"You want to talk about what happened back there?"

"Not really."

"Should we be worried?"

"I don't know. I hope I was imagining things."

"Your face was whiter than the snow falling out there. You had to have seen something."

"More like, heard."

He stared at me for a second before asking, "Well, what did you hear?"

I shook my head. "Snorting."

"So, it was a polar bear?"

"Yeah. I bet that's what it was."

"You're being a dick, William."

"Come on, Tom, give him a break," Tish said.

"You guys don't think we should know what the hell is going on?"

"Seriously, I don't know what it was. I heard something, or thought I did. I got scared and ran away pissing and crying. I'm sorry I scared you guys."

He just gave me a blank stare. I'm not sure he believed me, but then, I wasn't sure I believed what I'd said. I didn't really have time to reflect on what exactly had happened. I knew I'd heard something, and that I'd had some weird primal response to it, but I just didn't know. Everything was a blur.

Changing the subject, I asked, "How much farther, you think?"

"Maybe twenty minutes," Tom said.

"Good. I'll be glad to get off this godforsaken ice."

"Sorry for being an ass."

"It's all good. I'm sorry for being a pussy."

Tom laughed. "You should've seen yourself. You looked like The Michelin Man... if he were a little heavier and high on PCP and running from the cops."

"Jesus, Tom. Tell me how you really feel."

It would've been twenty minutes had things gone to plan. We spun a track on a steep section of a snowbank. An argument ensued between Titouan and Tom. Titouan told him he was being careless. Tom threatened to Kill Titouan if he said one more word. I was exhausted and had no patience for Titouan's bullshit. If Titouan had said one more word, I would've let Tom do whatever the hell he wanted. Luckily for Titouan, he decided to shut up for once.

"Looks like we're hoofin it, boys," Sam said, trying to cut through the tension.

Tom kicked the side of the Shining and said, "I didn't say anything when we left the patch, but I worried about the right track. It had seen better days, for sure."

Titouan began to say something, but I stopped him. "Dammit. Just shut the hell up. You can tell your dad paid your way into Wharton because you're dumb as shit, aren't you?"

"Son, you better listen to William. He's tryin to save ya from a bruisin," Sam said.

Titouan mumbled gibberish before grabbing his lantern and taking off in a direction he thought we should be going. After he thought he was outside of earshot, he muttered something more loudly than maybe he'd intended. Tom didn't take very kindly to having his mom being called a bitch. To my surprise, though, he just shook his head and laughed before saying, "I want to be in the room when he tells Miley what happened at the Patch."

I nodded. "We can make that happen."

There were no signs or geographical references like mountains to guide us in the right direction, and, honestly, it wouldn't have mattered if there had been. Mother Nature was throwing so much snow at us that with the bright lights of the Shining we could only see just a few feet in front of us. With our battery-powered lamps, it was much less; inches maybe. Factor in the windswept snow quickly obscuring the already deteriorating remnants of ice road, and what you had was a cluster-fuck in the making.

Tom thought the road wasn't a straight shot to Barrow. He believed it bent significantly to the east. We decided we'd rather miss Barrow to the west than to the east because it was so sparsely populated. We set out on a point roughly west of the front end of the Shining. If we had already left the road, we were screwed, plain and simple.

"What do we do about him?" Tish nodded her head towards Titouan. His little tantrum had netted him about twenty steps.

"He'll get back in line before he loses sight of our lamplight. He's too big of a pussy to go at it alone," Tom said, "especially now that he's seen a boogieman."

"This way, Titouan," I finally said. There was safety in numbers. He slowly adjusted his course but stayed back just far enough to try to make us believe he was still going his way.

We walked for what seemed like forever but still hadn't reached Barrow. The bit of good news was the gale-force winds had started to abate, if only a little, and so had the snowfall. Avery was the first one to say we should've seen lights from Barrow if we were even remotely close to it. That was the bad news. There were, however, clear signs of a snowbank to our left. Whether it was man-made or a product of the wind piling the snow was still up for debate. Nevertheless, we walked towards it.

"This is the road," Tom said. Avery agreed.

"Holy squirtin, Mother Mary, do ya guys see what I see?" Sam asked.

That happiness evident in Sam's characteristically crass retort quickly faded to apprehension as we got closer to the edge of town. Off beyond the rough banks of the seawall, I saw a smattering of small structures still mostly cloaked in darkness and blowing snow, but slowly coming into frame as we moved closer. Something odd soon became evident about those structures and the light poles dotting the road beside them, but also went a long way in explaining why we didn't see lights in Barrow. There weren't any. The town was dark.

Chapter 5

Barrow is a Jekyll and Hyde kind of city. If you were to walk the streets, seeing all the wind-battered and tattered houses, all the junk lying around, not to mention the unpaved roads, you might leave with the impression that it was one of the most forsaken and impoverished places you've ever seen. Take a closer look, and you might be surprised by what you uncover. You'll see schools that are equally as nice, and in some cases nicer, than most back in the lower forty-eight; libraries and administrative buildings that are also top-notch, and rounded off with many valuable services offered to the community. All of this wouldn't be possible if it weren't for the glut of oil revenues that flowed through Barrow, and, well, Alaska in general.

The bleak emptiness battered our spirits worse than the buffeting winds that assaulted us as we passed over the sea wall. There was no one in the streets but us. Our headlamps danced in the darkness, trying to find any sign that our initial reaction had just been carryover pessimism from the Patch. Tom tried in vain on at least three occasions to rouse people from their houses by pounding on their doors. There were no answers.

The Hyde side of Barrow was on full display.

Sam pointed to a group of small houses. "You see anythang odd 'bout 'em?"

"The doors are open," I said.

"Lot of houses with the doors wide open. Some shit goin on 'ere."

"Lot of that going on right now. Shit, that is."

Sam cocked his head, grinned, and said, "We should of done stayed in East Texas."

"No argument here."

Tish led us. Because she did her clinicals in Barrow, she had a much better idea about the lay of the land. She'd become invaluable as a member of our crew, even before the power had gone out. It's funny to think that she almost hadn't come to the Patch.

The day I called her for an interview, she'd said she'd been packing to go back to Fairbanks. She was finishing up her clinicals when she'd gotten into it with one of her advisers. The lady at the hospital had told me not to hire her because she was hateful, but I'd needed someone to help our nurse. Not taking the woman's advice, I'd interviewed her, and we hit it off instantly. We were glad to have her then, and we were gladder to have her that first night in Barrow.

We had just crossed over Stevenson Street and were making our way southeast to Momeganna Street. That would take us to the Wiley Post-Will Rogers Airport. Miley's office complex was about a mile to the east from there. We were already several blocks into the city by this point and still hadn't come across anything to ease the fears that something ominous and strange was happening. It was going to be a long, weird walk to Miley's.

"Must be about midday," Tish said.

I hadn't noticed until that moment that it had gotten a little brighter outside. Twilight isn't just a movie about douchey, brooding teenage vampires. It's also a time in the arctic winter (around noontime, or a bit earlier) when the sun is oriented just below the horizon but high enough to provide enough light to keep everything from being drenched in complete darkness. Depending on the time of year, it might last two or three hours. The extra light it brought was welcomed, indeed.

"At least we know about what time it is. That's something," I said.

Titouan sighed. "Does it really matter?"

"To us, it does."

"I guess."

"We'll just haft ta make the best of thangs, fellers," Sam said as he hurried to catch up with Tish.

Shaking his head, Titouan asked, "What's he got to be positive about?"

"The converse could be said about you," I said, smirking.

"Something is wrong with him if he can be happy during this," he said.

"The difference between you and Sam is he's not trying to bring people down. He's trying to help. You could learn a thing or two from him. Hell, we both could," I said.

He exhaled loudly, and slowed his pace so I would walk ahead of him.

I couldn't shake the feeling that we were being watched. During the entirety of that period, there weren't any noises or obvious indications that would warrant a normal person like I supposedly was to call for a full-on red alert. Still, I had a deep, visceral feeling lurking in the darkness. Obviously, with the hunt for Titouan's ghost episode not that far in the past, I didn't want to be fat-dude who cried wolf. Even when I finally heard real evidence, I was hesitant to act.

I slowed down. Avery synchronized his pace with mine but was seemingly oblivious as to why I'd slowed my pace. I gave him a glance, hoping he'd heard it, too. His eyes remained forward, though. He was there, but we were focused on different things; not to mention him apparently not hearing what I thought I had. We walked further, my head on a swivel, watching every alleyway and nook and cranny we passed. I saw nothing.

A bit further down the street, Avery gasped and blurted way too loudly, "William..." He turned to me, and with wide eyes, said, "Someone was crouched back there. I do not think he saw us. He seemed to be focused on something behind us."

Before I had time to react, I heard a loud sniff and a grunt, followed by fast footfalls from somewhere close behind. I turned to warn Tom. Too late. A gray blur was on him.

I watched Tom raise his rifle and try to aim, but he'd hesitated. A terrible scream exploded out of Tom's lungs as he hit the ground in a thud.

As quickly as it had begun, it was over. The man eyed me before settling his gaze on Avery. His eyes stayed there too long. So long, I thought he might try to attack Avery next. I positioned myself in front of him, but the man's attention waned. His eyes fell to Tom's one last time before standing. His head then jerked inhumanly towards a side street. He fell into a hard run in that direction, leaving Tom lying in the street.

Sam caught up to and passed me on his way to our fallen friend. As I neared Tom, I heard him say, "The sonofabitch cut me."

I gasped at what I saw: crimson flowed through the gaps between his fingers as he grasped his throat.

Curses and hard breaths filled the space formerly occupied by the howling wind and pelting snow.

"He's bleedin bad, boys," Sam said.

Tish didn't waste any time. She rummaged through her bag. Frustrated, she said something about not having what she needed to help him. How do you like that? —we brought a nurse but forgot things she might need in an emergency. A case study in how not to handle emergencies. I picked up the gun and prepared to guard against another attack. Maybe I could at least do that right.

"How bad is it?" I asked, trying to keep a lookout while struggling to get my breath.

She didn't respond.

"Is he dying?" Avery asked.

"Shut yer damn mouth, boy," Sam hissed.

"Apply pressure here, Sam. We have to get him inside, and quickly," Tish said, and wiped the blood on her pants.

I knew we had to get him inside, but inside where? We were still more than a mile from Miley's office. Assuming the hospital was operational, and I didn't, it was farther than Miley's. That also wouldn't work. Instead of concentrating on what I needed to do, my mind raced about things I should've done differently in my life, both past and present.

I heard a voice off in the distance; faint but serious. Was that what a nervous breakdown felt like? I reasoned, if I was cognizant enough to question my mental state, then I probably wasn't. I'm not sure you have the faculty of recognition during an episode such as this, but I might've been overthinking things.

The voice called again, louder this time, yet muffled and incomprehensible. If you've ever watched a war movie; the voice sounded like what a soldier hears after an explosion. After some time, I decided it was Tish's voice. She was yelling at me. Instantly, the world snapped back into focus.

On sheer instinct, I ran down Nanook Street. The first or second house I came to, I ran up and kicked the door in. I don't even remember checking if it was unlocked. I just kicked the hell out of it, over and over until it swung wide open. I called warnings to anyone who might be inside then waited. No one, thankfully, answered.

I busted ass back to Tom, sweat pouring off me as my feet pounded the snow. As tired and out of breath as I was, I managed to help Sam carry Tom back to the broken-in house.

"Easy," Tish said, as we gently lay him on the living room floor.

"Figure out how to keep that door closed, Avery," I said, hands on knees and gulping for breaths that weren't coming quickly enough. And if that wasn't a testament to how out of shape I was, I don't know what is. I remember being told in peewee football to stand up straight and put my hands on my head. I did that now, and it seemed to help. I was dizzy as hell and coughed until I nearly puked. I needed to lose some damn weight.

We placed lamps around Tom. His face was already pale from loss of blood. He worked his mouth, attempting to say something, but nothing came out. His eyelids fluttered and then slid closed, hopefully just passing out from loss of blood or pain and not anything more grievous. Tish grabbed a pillowcase off a pillow on the couch to replace the blood-soaked bandage she'd applied earlier. It didn't seem particularly sterile, but I didn't argue. "Keep the pressure, Sam," Tish said, placing his hand where hers was.

Tish pulled me aside. As much as she tried to hide it, she looked terrified.

"William," she whispered, through trembling lips, "I'm not sure I can help him. I'm... I'm not ready for this."

"None of us are. We have to do the best we can. That's all we can do."

Tears streamed down her face. "It could be his carotid artery..."

"Then, you probably need to be working on it."

She nodded slightly and wiped her eyes and nose with her ungloved hands. "I have to have needle and thread to stitch up his neck."

I searched through an adjoining bedroom and heard Titouan say something to the extent that we should we worry about the homeowner returning.

"You'll have a lot more ta worry 'bout if you don't get ta lookin for what Tish needs."

I opened a door in the bedroom that, weirdly, led into the kitchen. I pulled out every drawer I saw. I was looking for the one drawer that rules them all. The one that is stuffed full of crap like menus from every restaurant in town, tools of various types, potholders, and the two things we needed most: needle and thread.

After a few minutes, I found what I was looking for. "I'll be damned," I said aloud. "Everyone does have that drawer." Even in Alaska.

Needle and thread in hand, I began to hurry out of the kitchen when I saw something out of place near the table. The battery in my headlamp was nearly dead, so it was difficult to make out the form in the shadows of the dark kitchen. I inched towards the table, where a human-shaped silhouette began to take form. I came to a dead stop. Holy shit.

"I'm so sorry for being in here," I said. "Our friend is hurt. I didn't think anyone was home..." I stopped, leaving plenty of space between myself and the table. I could now see the form of who was sitting there, but the shadows concealed whether it was male or female, and honestly, to me, it didn't matter. I was an intruder in someone's home, in Alaska, the place where everyone has a gun.

"Hello?" No answer. I lowered the gun barrel, taking as passive of a stance as possible. For all I knew, the person had been pointing a gun pointed at me since I'd entered the kitchen, and my life hung on a single false step. "Hello," I repeated.

I adjusted my headlamp, hoping to get a better view of the person. It was a woman... Her eyes were wide open like she'd seen a ghost or something. "I'm sorry, I didn't mean to scare you," I said. Her mouth was closed, lips pinched so tightly there was scant difference between the upper and lower lips. My first inclination was that she was dead. There was a newspaper and a half-empty glass of water on the table beside her.

Maybe she'd had an aneurysm or something—just died while reading the morning paper.

Feeling comfortable enough in this assessment, I inched closer. Sam's voice could be heard from the living room. Tish's, too. They were talking about something, but I couldn't make out precisely what. It never entered my mind to call to them. Hell, I'd forgotten I had the needle and thread. My focus was squarely on the madness unfolding in the kitchen.

She seemed to be middle-aged, studious looking, and not unattractive—or was at some time in the near past, attractive. Those features were, however, completely overwhelmed by her other, more defining characteristics. Her skin was a sickly, blueish-gray, slippery, and shiny due to a layer of slimy film that covered her exposed flesh. Her eyes were dark and impossibly large for her face; or any face, for that matter. The whites of her eyes had been replaced with the same sickly gray color as her skin. Her irises and pupils were indistinguishable from one another and took up a disproportionate amount of space on her enlarged eyeballs.

I had never seen a dead person's eyes before, but not even in my most wicked of magic-mushroom driven dreams could I conjure up anything that remotely looked like hers.

A noise jolted me out of my nightmare. Something heavy had been knocked over in the snow outside the house—muted, but loud enough to send another wave of adrenaline through my saturated nervous system.

I hurried towards the window facing the backyard. Even with the extra light twilight afforded, the only thing I could see of note was a pile of broken appliances. The pale light from my lamp caused a glare on the windowpane, which further obscured the view out the window. I switched it off but still saw nothing that could've caused the noise. More ghosts, I thought.

As I had more pressing issues inside, I flipped my headlamp back on and returned my attention to the dead lady at the kitchen table.

Something I was pretty sure was impossible then happened—for a dead person, anyway. I quickly turned out the lamp as worried utterings carried into the kitchen from the living room. After a second or two, I flicked my headlamp back on. Her left pupil seemed to dilate. Dead people's eyes don't tend to do that, and they sure as hell don't blink.

Even as fear and uncertainly gripped me in its bony pinchers, I moved a step closer. An eyelid fluttered. Another step closer, and I heard a faint moan fight to escape her tightly-pinched lips. I stopped, but what I really wanted to do was run. Get as far away from that thing as I could, because she was not dead. As if to verify that theory for me, her cheek twitched violently while she strained to motivate her one mobile eyeball into a sideways glance towards me.

Another noise. This time inside the kitchen. Footsteps: their owner, a shadow-cloaked figure, skulked towards me. Acting on pure instinct, and only having a few rational brain cells in the fight, I swung the rifle around to greet my assailant.

Much of that encounter was drowned in adrenaline and pure unadulterated fear. I do, however, remember hearing Titouan's voice while taking aim at my attacker. Too bad for Titouan, my brain didn't register the possibility the recognized voice might be inextricably connected to the still veiled figure.

Aside from the trigger pull, which happened at the speed of light, everything moved in a poor man's version of a Matrix-inspired, bullet-time-esque, shootout. Poor man's because it was my dumb ass pulling the trigger. I remember the single flash from the muzzle and the smell of cordite that ensued. I also remember Titouan screaming.

"Goddamn you, William! You fucking shot me!"

I didn't kill him. Dead people didn't run, but their eyes weren't supposed to blink either, so who knew. Either way, he took off towards the living room, holding the right side of his face.

"Shit." I couldn't believe I'd shot him.

"Fucking bastard shot me," he said from the living room.

Sam told Titouan, "It's a damn scratch. You ain't goin ta die."

I was relieved by that. He was a dick, but I didn't want to kill him. Somebody would end up doing it, but I didn't want that person to me.

I felt someone tug at the gun. Avery of all people was who took the rifle from me.

"Are you okay?" Avery asked.

"Did you see her?"

Avery looked confused. "Her?"

"The woman sitting at the damn table!"

Avery raised his lamp to get a better look. "I do not see anyone."

Since my headlamp's battery was almost completely drained, and given how he wasn't shining the light in the right spot, I grabbed the lamp from Avery. I wasn't sure how it was possible, or if maybe I'd lost my mind, but the woman was no longer seated at the table. "She was sitting right there, dammit. Right there!" I pointing at the table.

"You are not well. Maybe you are suffering from delirium brought on by our current—"

"Shut up!" Seeing the confused look form on Avery's face, I moderated my tone. "Please, just shut up for a minute."

I walked around to the back of the table and saw her lying on the floor, obscured by the table and the dim light from Avery's also-drained lamp. "I told you she was sitting there. I'm not fucking crazy."

The impact I felt as I wheeled the gun around was me bashing the side of the woman's skull with the end of the barrel. I hit her so hard that I knocked her out of the chair and onto the floor. The problem was she was lying in the same position she'd been in while sitting in the chair. I grabbed her hand, but it rubber-banded back into the same pronated position it'd been previously.

"She is dead, William."

"Unless I killed her when I hit her with the barrel, I don't believe that to be true."

"That is impossible." He nudged her arm with the barrel of the gun, but as soon as the barrel was removed, her arm bounced back into position. "She smells dead. She has rigor mortis. She is dead."

I'm not sure why I did what I did next. I spun her around on the floor until she faced me. I then bent over and picked her up, but because she was covered in the slippery substance, she kept sliding out of my grasp. Determined, I wiped the film covering her exposed skin on my pants and grasped her around her waist. Avery whispered a prayer as I struggled to put her back in the chair. Sucking breaths and dizzy from my manic episode, I nearly knocked the lamp off the table as I swung her once more towards the chair. She had tears in her eyes and wet trails down her cheeks.

I sniffed my mucous-covered hands. They smelled like fruit gone bad. Not exactly terrible, but you wouldn't want to wear that essence on a first date. There were some disinfectant wipes on the counter. I grabbed a ton of them and began violently wiping at my hands and coat, trying to remove as much of the slime as possible.

"Dead people cannot cry, William," Avery said, snapping his fingers.

She began to whimper. "They don't do that either," I reiterated.

Avery dreamed of moments like we were experiencing: an authentic unexplainable incident, and what does he do? He tucks tale and full-on runs into the living room, uttering more prayers to God and all his saints. I followed him, hoping some of the prayers would be answered. I was desperate.

"Now, what in the world is wrong with him? Hell, you both done look like you seen a ghost," Sam said, as he finished cleaning up Titouan's wounded face.

"Try to kill him, too?" Titouan snarled.

"Not fucking now," I told him.

"Son, what's 'at noise in 'ere?" Sam asked.

"The dead woman," Avery blurted, as he rocked back and forth on the couch.

Sam walked over to where Avery sat and grabbed the rifle. "Neither of you'ins gets to hold 'is for a while. Stop being crazy, and I'll give y'all 'nother chance," he said, eyeing both me and Avery. "Now, let's see what the hell is goin on in 'at kitchen."

Avery began to pray: first barely audible, then growing louder and louder.

"What the hell are you doing, Avery?" Titouan asked.

"Currently, I am invoking my Lord God through his Son, God Dammit."

I led Sam and Tish into the kitchen. Avery and Titouan stayed in the living room. One nursed his cut and burned face while the other one—well, he was busy talking to God through Jesus. Whatever kept them out of our hair while we figured what the hell was going on was fine by me.

"Oh my God," Tish said, as the woman continued whimpering.

Tish moved closer to her, cupping her mouth with a bloody hand. She placed two fingers on the woman's neck to check for a pulse. She shook her head, seemingly frustrated, before trying again. Finally, she wiped her fingers on her pants and said, "Besides the mucous, the smell, and the catatonic state, she's normal," Tish said.

I gave her a long look. There had to be more.

Apparently sensing my apprehension, she said, "Her pulse is a little slow but normal enough."

For whatever reason, I needed to let Tish know what I'd done. "I hit her with the rifle barrel before I shot Titouan."

She gave me a quick once over, then turned her attention back to the woman.

The woman blinked. This time, it was the other eye.

"Yeah," I said, trying to control my breaths. I was hyperventilating.

Sam grabbed her hand and lifted it. It fell exactly back into place where it rested on the table. "I'll take her out back and put her out of her damn misery. 'Is ain't right, son."

Her mouth was still clamped shut, but the whimpers were getting louder and louder, apparently to the point of being heard in the living room. Titouan stood in the kitchen doorway. "Shut that thing up. Jesus!"

Sam, seeing that Titouan was going to cause more problems, firmly led him back into the living room. "Just shut the hell up and stay in 'ere. 'Ey dealin with it."

"What do you think, Tish?" I asked.

Tish, no longer able to look at the woman sitting at the table, walked over to the kitchen window. I didn't tell her, but one of the woman's eyes, the same one that accosted me, seemed to track her as she moved past.

Wiping her eyes, Tish said after a few moments, "I don't know."

"We can't just leave her in here like this," I said.

"None of this makes any sense. This isn't supposed to be happening like this," Tish said, still looking out the window.

"What do you mean by that?" I asked.

Tish jerked her head towards me. "What?"

"What do you mean by 'not happening like this'?"

"I don't know. I'm just talking out of my head." She began to sob. "It's just..." She nodded towards the woman. "Her. It... her, none of this makes any sense."

"Maybe we should take the conversation in there," I said, not knowing if the woman was lucid enough to understand what we were saying. Maybe she would stop making the noises if we left, I thought. I really wanted her to stop.

"I need to check on Tom, anyway," she said, wiping the tears from her face.

Once we were in the living room, I asked her how he was doing.

"I stopped the bleeding. I hope, anyway. It wasn't as bad as I feared. We got lucky. It wasn't the carotid."

"I wasn't thinking. I should've told you something."

"What?" she asked.

Tom was taking a blood thinner. I knew this because he had a heart attack while we were eating supper back in East Texas. Some of the guys and I were the only people who went to see him at the hospital. We never talked about it, but I knew he had family back in Florida. For whatever reason, none of them cared enough to come or even call during his treatment and recovery. He never seemed too sad about it, and like I said, I didn't ask.

"He's on a blood thinner."

"That would've been nice to know."

"I can't believe he didn't tell you."

She gave me a strange look. "Yeah, well, he didn't tell me everything."

I didn't want to know where that rabbit hole led.

***

We'd been inside the house for several hours. The adrenaline had long ago diminished, leaving me with ragged nerves and exhaustion beyond anything I'd ever personally experienced. We needed rest, and even though the house was freezing, I, at least, didn't care.

Sam had a different idea, apparently born out of growing up in the Holler. He explained how his parents hung blankets to blocked off any unused space in the house because the small wood stove in the living room couldn't heat the entire home. It worked like a charm for us, as well. Once the doorways to the bedrooms, hallway, and kitchen were covered, the living room became nice and toasty.

We had a woodstove in the trailer I'd grown up in. If only my mom and any of my stepdads had been as innovative as Sam's parents. It was too hot in the living room, and too cold in the bedrooms. And, my god, was the bathroom cold. You let the hot water run for several minutes before you ever thought about taking your clothes off. God, what a great childhood that was.

The blankets covering the doorway also had a secondary benefit. They helped mute the woman's constant whimpering. That was until she began trying to sound out actual words. She kept repeating the letter t. "Tttttttt..." followed by more whimpering. Tish spent several moments in the kitchen checking on her. By the time she'd finished, the woman had gone quiet. No one asked how Tish managed that feat. It was quiet, and that was enough.

So, we wouldn't feel like complete dogs, we did agree that if she regained more movement, we would do everything in our power to help. I'm not sure if we meant it or not. If I'm being honest, we made that pact to make ourselves feel better about trying to ignore another human's suffering. And look, it was obvious by that point she was suffering, but we had no tools at our disposal in which to help her.

And even if we would've had the resources to help her, I wasn't sure it would've mattered. We had all seen the person who'd attacked Tom. We had all seen his gray skin—his gray face. There had to be some relation between him, the lady in the kitchen, and what was happening in Barrow. While none of us spoke about it, it was clear there had to be a connection.

If it weren't for Tom's injury, we would've already left that house. It was not safe there. Because of that, we decided that someone needed to stay away and keep watch. Sam decided he would go first because he didn't really trust any of us besides maybe Tish with the rifle. I personally didn't care. I was so tired I allowed myself to forget about the present dangers. I was asleep within minutes of my head hitting the pillow I'd taken from one of the bedrooms.

***

I opened my heavy eyes. I'd hoped I was just having a nightmare, but my aching back and sore knees were testament to how real things were. Sam gave me a perplexed look as I came to a sitting position on the floor. "How long did I sleep?"

"Accordin ta 'at damn grandfather clock over yonder, you was asleep 'bout three hours. I ain't sure how you slept past the damn ringin of 'em chimes."

He told me that at one point he'd nearly fallen asleep when the "damn thang went off and almost caused me ta pee my pants."

I told him I was good. I would take over for him. Exhaustion had worn him down to the point where he was willing to overlook his fear, as well. Well, not completely. "Don't shoot none us in our sleep, you crazy bastard." He slapped me on my uninjured shoulder and took occupancy of the pallet I'd just gotten up from. "You better not done farted under 'ese blankets."

"Way to keep it classy, Sam."

I sat in the chair by the small window. Enough cold air radiated off the windowpane to give a chill, but as exhausted as I was, it helped me stay awake. The snow had nearly stopped. And while twilight had long since given up its light, the full moon, coupled with a mostly cloudless sky, shined brightly enough I could see with decent clarity just beyond the street that ran parallel with the front of the house.

A broken-down car sat just off the street. It was elevated on blocks, waiting for whatever parts it needed. But then the car could've also been a complete piece of junk. Because everything in Barrow was so damn expensive, people rarely threw anything away, especially vehicles. That was why there was so much junk scattered everywhere.

I couldn't help myself from wishing the car was operable. I would've liked to have jumped in and driven as far away as possible. That wouldn't have been that far. There were no roads that led to any other city in Alaska out of Barrow. Unless you had a tracked vehicle or an airplane, you were stuck. Still, anywhere aside from inside that house sounded damn fine to me.

Since I couldn't escape in the broken-down beater in the front yard, I'd settle for a different kind of escape. I had accidentally brought a snack with me—remnants of a late-night, binge-eating session from a few days prior. I took the candy bar out of my coat pocket and began eating it. The sugar was magic. It made me instantly feel better. I was finishing the last bite when I heard Tom say something in a raspy but understandable voice. "Did you save me some, you fat bastard?"

"If I'd known you weren't dead, I would've," I replied with a big grin. Damn, I was glad to hear his voice.

"You think I can get a drink? My throat feels like sandpaper."

"Bourbon, maybe?"

"God, that would be great."

"Yeah, well, you're probably going to have to settle for water."

"Story of my life," he croaked.

As quietly as I could, I rummaged through our bags, looking for a bottle of water. I cursed under my breath as I realized we didn't have anymore. "I'll be back in second. I'll grab some from the kitchen."

The kitchen, I remember thinking. I sighed as I pulled aside the blankets that were draped over the doorway and entered. Once in the kitchen, I couldn't stop myself from stealing psychologically expensive glances towards the woman. Trust me, I tried to stop myself. I wanted to not see her. But the cat was out of the bag. I had seen her. I had seen what Tish had done to her to make her quiet.

And while I was momentarily upset by what I saw, the duct-tape covering her mouth had quieted her. No cries or whimpering from her allowed me—us—to forget about her being in the cordoned-off room. That coinciding with the very real yet unknown threat awaiting us outside those walls made it much easier for formerly-caring humans to give too much of a damn about her.

No, I wasn't mad at Tish for what she'd done.

There was a pitcher of water in the fridge. I grabbed a cup from the drainer and proceeded to fill it, cursing the Gods for every extra second I spent in there.

Tom sat up. He took several long drafts from the cup before lying back down. He fiddled with the bandage on the side of his neck.

"Hurts like hell," he said.

Tish said whoever cut him had used a dull knife. The wound was not a straight, quick cut. It was more a tear than anything. If the person had used a sharp knife, he likely would've killed him. Tom didn't need to know the details. "I bet."

"What the hell happened?"

"You don't remember?"

"Obviously, some asshole cut me, but I don't remember much after that."

"We don't know what happened either. Whoever did it ran away. Didn't even steal anything from you."

"Didn't have much to steal." Tom looked around the room before settling on me; befuddled by what he saw, he asked, "Where the hell are we?"

"Good question. Just somebody's house we broke into."

"Keeps getting better."

He lay back down for a minute or two because he felt sick to his stomach. After the queasiness had passed, he proceeded to tell me some of what he was beginning to remember. He said he'd noticed a house with its door wide open. "Who leaves a door open like that when it's this cold? Something wasn't right about it. It was just a feeling I had, you know. Then—"

"There's nothing right about what's happening."

"Then I heard thumping inside. Like people were wrestling." Against his better judgment, he said he'd been about to yell inside to see if everything was okay. He was about to do so when he heard sniffing just inside the open door. "First thing that came to mind was dogs—big bastards. I don't know what was going on inside, but you don't go messing with dogs like that. I said the hell with that, you know what I'm saying?"

He coughed. "You think I can get some more water? My throat is fucked."

I walked quickly past her. I hurriedly refilled the glass and hauled ass back to Tom, without even a glance in her direction. I handed Tom the glass, and he gulped it down. He coughed a few more times, shook his head, and told me he didn't feel well.

"Maybe it's time to get some more rest," I told him.

He shook his head, letting me know he wanted to continue. "I was about to catch up with you guys when I heard something behind me. I raised my lamp but didn't see anything. As I turned back around, though, I saw the guy charging me like a crazed bull. I dropped the lamp..."

Tom got quiet for a few moments. Not quite like he was lost in thought. He was not well. That much was blatantly obvious. "I'm dizzy as hell, man," he said, coming to rest on an elbow.

"We'll talk about this crap later. You need to rest, man."

"I got a good look at him before he attacked me." He coughed and then swallowed hard, his Adam's Apple, bobbing downward and then back to its original position. "Yeah, I don't feel good. I'm going to take a breather."

Tom never complained about any of the procedures he'd gotten over the years. Seeing him like that was tough. "Yeah, you do that. Can I get you anything?"

"No," he said weakly.

He tossed and turned a couple times before going completely quiet. He didn't even snore, which was odd, because he was notorious for his snoring. It was so bad he was the only person who didn't have to share a room with anyone at the nest. Everyone to a man refused to be his bunkmate. Sam said, "He gotta be fakin 'em noises, cause ain't no human makin' 'em on accident. Bastard wonts his own room. 'At's all it was."

My body ached all over. My legs and lower back hurt the most. I stood up for a moment, thinking stretching would be a worthwhile idea. It wasn't. After deciding the pain caused by stretching rigid muscles was worse than not doing anything at all, I fell back into the uncomfortable chair. It groaned under my weight. Thankfully, it stayed in one piece.

It might seem odd, but I'd been in that house for several hours by then, but it was only during that moment, as I kneaded my sore leg muscles, that I paid any attention to my surroundings. I was struck by just how barren the living room was. The place looked like it wasn't lived in. It was devoid of anything that made a house a home. There were no pictures, knickknacks; nothing you might expect. There was a small television, the grandfather clock, a love seat, and two worn-out chairs. One of which was the one I occupied.

Out of the corner of my eye, I saw movement in the yard. A man came to a stop near the broken-down car. "What the hell?" I muttered to myself, barely above a whisper.

He fell on his haunches before turning his nose skyward. I'm not sure why or how, but he was shirtless, for sure. I was less certain about whether he had anything on his feet. It was hard to see because of the snow cover. My first inclination was that he had to be freezing to death out there, but I saw little evidence of that being the case. I took a hard look at Avery's jerry-rigged door and prayed to the gods it might hold if this guy decided he wanted inside.

I glanced at the rifle I'd leaned against the wall near the chair. I hoped I wouldn't need to use it.

Having turned my attention away from my fear of using the weapon and the man's clothing choices, I realized we were in trouble. His skin was the same gray color as the lady in the kitchen. His eyes... they were the same, too: inhumanly large, and black as onyx. The only discernible difference between the two was his mobility.

He began sniffing so loudly, I heard it from inside the house. His head jerked back towards the street. He bellowed out a guttural wail so loud half of Barrow would hear it, which, as I would soon find out, was the point.

After a couple minutes, I heard crunching footsteps outside the house, followed soon after by visual evidence in the form of a tall—and this time fully dressed—figure emanated from the side of the house. She came to a stop near the still squatting man. She would not be the last. Over the next ten or so minutes, the front yard became a gathering place for the gray things. In all, I counted twenty-one Grays. Far too many for us to take on had they decided to make trouble. Why else would they be there? And why were they outside?

Had it been one of those things who'd attacked Tom? Why? What the hell had happened to them? It wasn't the fault of a stroke or aneurysm, as I'd tricked myself into believing was the issue with the lady in the kitchen. It was those kinds of contemplations that helped me to stumble my way into recognizing how things were exponentially worse than downtime, lost earnings at the Patch, a city-wide power outage in Barrow, or even an assault on my good friend. No, this was much worse than those things, combined. I would've bet the farm on it. Well, the seventy-nine Starlight house trailer, in my case.

Of course, not even neon signs, blinking their garish displays, could've warned me to the fact that the world had shifted radically under my feet, rendering much of what I'd known as useless as believing Sam's story about being abducted by aliens. As terrible—not to mention, as obvious—as the ailments plaguing kitchen-lady clearly were, it was unacceptable to come to any conclusion about her condition other than a default notion of whatever it is, it shouldn't diverge too far from orthodoxy. That's why, even as her alien eyes leaked tears, my initial impression had been that it had to be something as obvious as an aneurysm. Not that I really knew exactly what the hell an aneurysm was, other than it was something people died from every day; but, it was known, and so it didn't take much of a leap for a layperson like me to accept as fact and move on.

The problem with that type of thinking was it would get you killed. The radical winds had blown in a storm, and we had no clue how to save ourselves. That's why we hadn't spent another second trying to fortify the door Avery had barely secured. Why would we? What was the worst that would happen? The angry owner might come home and, what, call the police? There were no police; or, at that point, sure as hell didn't seem to be. If we were going to live, we would need to learn an entirely new rulebook. In the process of learning that rulebook, you wouldn't get a fine if you broke a rule. You would die.

I was so absorbed with everything that raced across my mind, and the gathering outside, I hadn't even noticed Sam coming to stand beside me. "Jesus, son... What in the damn Sam Hill is 'is shit?"

"We're fucked."

Chapter 6

"We're sitting ducks in here, William," Titouan said.

I sucked in a breath and sighed, thinking about what not to say, before deciding on, "I'm open to reasonable ideas."

"Run out the back door and get our asses to Miley's as fast as we can."

"Reasonable ideas, I said. What happens to Tom in your little plan?"

"The greater good," he replied, stumbling slightly over his words.

"Don't give me that greater-good bullshit. There's nothing great or good about it."

"Tit, me and you disagree on 'bout everthang, and 'is sure as hell ain't no different. I can't believe 'at even you thanks 'at's a option," Sam said, rubbing his hands together next to the heater. "Tom's a good man. We can't just leave 'im here like a pile of trash."

"It's not about what's best for me. It's about what's best for all of us," he said.

"Since when have you ever cared 'bout 'is us thang you talkin 'bout?"

"We have a moral dilemma," Avery said.

"No, we have a dickhead dilemma," I said.

Avery snapped his fingers while saying, "But Titouan makes a valid point. If we stay, we might all die. If we leave Tom, we could very well escape and live."

"This isn't a classroom, Avery. We don't get to flex our creative minds while exploring fucking existentialism in the abstract. Tom is as real as that seat your ass is planted in. We're not leaving him. Drop it."

Titouan glanced at Avery before saying, "This is just the way it is. You may not like it, but if we take Tom, it makes the rest of us weaker."

"Titouan, if you were in the same predicament, I wouldn't leave you behind either. I don't know what's going on, but we—" I pointed at each one of them "—are all we've got right now. We've got to stick together."

Titouan shrugged and focused his attention elsewhere.

"What's that noise?" Tish said, breaking the silence that had settled into the room.

Avery slowly turned his head towards me, his eyes big as half dollars.

There was a rhythmic tapping coming from the bedroom adjoining the living room. I quietly walked over to Tish and said, "I'm going see what the hell that is. I need you to try to get Tom up, and, if possible, ready to leave."

She nodded.

I glanced out the living room window. For whatever reason, those things had become agitated.

"Take the rifle," Sam said.

"No. Keep it in here." I flicked my chin in the direction where the things were outside. "You at least know how to use it."

With the snow having almost abated, and with the full moon casting its light through the bedroom window, I saw it as soon as I entered the bedroom: first, on the floor, in the form of a long shadow, but also as a large, human-shaped silhouette in the window. "Mother of God," I uttered. Paralyzed with fear, I moved no further than the steps I'd already taken.

The person kept an eerie beat as he tapped his forehead against the windowpane, repeatedly. And then, the tapping stopped. Instead, the man pressed the side of his face against the glass, his nose facing in my direction. He sniffed several times before going still. The condensation from his rapid exhalations formed frost on a section of the glass. At the same time, his droopy folds of gray skin were pressed so hard against the glass, it looked like a small piece of Play-doh spread too thinly by a rolling pin. Without warning, and without any tell as to why he did what he did, he began tapping his forehead anew.

"William, you gonna want ta come in 'ere," Sam said.

Again, the man stopped. "Shh!" I hissed. He sniffed and then snorted loudly before once again tapping at the window. Except this time, he pounded. The window was about to be a thing of the past.

A cacophony of noise erupted in the living room, punctuated with Sam yelling for me to get my ass in there. Sam's yelling had the effect of causing the headbanger guy to increase the force of his banging. "Shit," I said as I turned away from the window.

I ran out of the bedroom, nearly tripping over a rug as I entered the living room. Upon regaining my balance, I saw Tom standing roughly where he'd been lying. He was doubled over, his arms cinched hard around his stomach. His face was contorted in a mixture of terror and pain, as he moaned and gurgled sickly noise, a frothy-dark mixture flowed from the corners of his mouth and down his face and neck.

Tish backed away from Tom. His torturous moans subsided as he tracked her retreat. The look of pain and fear so vividly displayed on his face just moments earlier were gone, replaced instead by an emotionally muddled visage that, all at once, had his lips pursed into a smile; the dark remnants from whatever crap flowed from his mouth had stained an angry frown on his face.

Tish and Tom locked glances. Tom's lips seem to quiver, the last vestiges of his humanity fall away as his eyes begin to flutter. He grasped his face, cried out, as a new wave of pain assaulted him.

Avery pointed to something outside. His mouth moved, but he wasn't saying anything—not anything that resembled recognizable speech, anyway.

There were now fists pounding on the front door.

A crash in the bedroom—the window. Headbanger was not alone. More sounds resonated through the house: shattered panes and strewn shards, floorboards groaning underfoot. And thuds from bodies pouring in through the windows. The bastards were inside.

My eyes flicked back to Tom, who seemed to have escaped the grip of pain that had engulfed him only seconds earlier. He turned towards me. In a primal voice, I barely recognized as my own, I cried out in confusion and sadness. I don't even know what I said, or if I said anything at all. Maybe, I screamed. I don't know.

His head jerked away randomly like it wasn't sure what it should be looking at, before momentarily settling back in my direction. In the dim light, I saw his eyes—eyes that just moments ago were normal and filled with life. As his gaze settled once more on mine, I saw the transition was complete. Tom was gone.

The thing that had taken control of his body tilted his head slightly to the side and sniffed. His head then jerked towards the kitchen and once again at me. I wasn't under any impression that Tom was stealing glances at me because he cared or even recognized me. That ship had sailed. He was looking for something to attack.

"Dear Jesus," Sam said.

My mind raced in an infinite loop of uncertainty. Nothing made sense. Tom's eyes weren't supposed to look like that. The eyes I knew were full of life. The ones I saw now were alien. A loud noise broke my trance. I turned towards it just as I saw, out of the corner of my eye, Tom sprinting towards the kitchen.

The front door gave way, and more bodies filled the house. Without a weapon, I was powerless to stop the mass of attackers flooding into the living room. The slow, unsure sounds of footsteps coming from the bedroom, the site of the loud noise of crashing glass, became fast and deliberate as headbanger sprinted through the living room and towards the kitchen, knocking me hard to the ground in the process. The side of my face bore most of the impact, and I momentarily lost consciousness.

I began to come to, which, considering how things were before I lost consciousness, couldn't have been more than a minute, I tried to sit. After much struggle, I had placed my ass firmly on the floor.

I blinked and squinted to see in the low light of the living room. I reached for the switch on my headlamp, but my fine motor movements hadn't yet come online. Your brain smacking against your skull will do that. I flicked my fingers and flexed my hand before trying again. Success: I could see.

I scanned the room. Having never moved, Avery sat in the chair in front of the window. He seemed frozen in place, like a goat, fearing for its life. Tish had been knocked down in the carnage as well, and Sam was at her side making sure she was okay. Everyone was accounted for except Titouan.

I flicked my head around the room, frantic for any sign of him. I was about to try to stand when I found him no more than a couple of arm-lengths away. Motionless and locked into a losing battle with shock, he watched—or, at least, was going through the motion of watching—whatever was happening inside the kitchen.

Jesus, the kitchen. My brain, consciousness, or maybe even my heart, refused to accept the stimuli pouring like a turbo-charged sieve out of the kitchen. The grotesque sounds assaulted my senses, as I battled an uncooperative body on a second front. Something terrible was taking place inside that kitchen. The monsters, the Grays, were eating the woman. Her muffled screams overrode all other data points. And if they were eating her, they would also try to eat us if we let them. I had to get up and get moving.

Knees wobbled, and I felt dizzier than if I'd just gotten off a tilt-a-whirl powered by crack. "We have to get the hell out of here," I said, placing my left hand on the couch for support.

Sam took a couple quick steps towards the door before stopping. "What 'bout Tom?"

"What about him?" I asked. Hadn't he seen what I had?

Sam shook his head and had begun to speak when Avery, with no urging from anyone, ran to the center of the room and started packing our belongings. He kneeled, feverishly tossing items into a large backpack, while never averting his eyes away from the black vortex that was the kitchen.

"Sam," I said, as I tossed my backpack over my shoulder. "Grab your shit, now."

He blinked, shook his head, growled, and began scooping up some of he and Tish's things before moving towards the exit, Tish in tow. Avery was right on his heels, things falling out of his haphazardly packed bag, as he stumbled his way outside.

I'd gathered what I could and began my own retreat when it occurred to me Titouan must've been in shock. His gaze had never left the kitchen. I cast my headlamp towards his morbid fixation. Hearing it was bad enough.

There was a marked decrease in noise level after I shined my light into the kitchen. Very stupid, I thought.

"Titouan," I whispered. "Let's go."

A fight broke out in the kitchen. One of the rooted-out Grays turned his blood-soaked face towards the living room and had taken too many steps towards us when I decided it was time to use a different tactic. Words weren't working. He flinched as I grabbed his arm. For a solitary moment, he acted as though he might pull away. I shook my head. He seemed to relax slightly after that. I grabbed his bag, tossed it over his shoulder, and we were halfway to the road when I saw Sam walking towards us.

He stopped me in the middle of the road. "What 'bout Tom?"

"Let's go, Sam."

"We gonna just leave him."

"Yes. Now, let's fucking hurry," I said, making sure no Grays had left the house.

"Well, I ain't leavin him," Sam insisted.

I ushered Titouan and Avery along, while I walked back towards where Sam stood in the middle of the street. "We can talk about this when we get the hell away from here," I said. "Were you not inside the same house I was?"

Sam glanced towards Tish, who had not stuck around. He frowned as he said, "We ain't never goin ta forget any of what done happened tanight. Hope you know 'at shit."

"No arguments here, Sam." I glanced towards Tish, who had, by then, almost made it to Momegonna Street, a good fifty yards or so away. I could tell he was bothered by her leaving him. I could also tell he didn't like that he might not be able to get to her quickly enough if something were to happen. Without uttering another word, making eye contact, or even grunting in my direction, he took off at a decent clip in her direction.

We ran south on Momeganna Street until we made a left on Ahkovak Street. By the time we reached Wiley Post-Will Roger's Airport, we were all winded and in need of a break.

"What now?" I huffed, struggling for every breath.

Clearly not happy, Sam said, between his own ragged breaths, "What the hell did we just do, leavin Tom like 'at?"

"Lived," I said.

"Tom was sick, you sonofabitch. For you ta be a bastard like 'at 'bout it—"

"Fucking hell," Titouan said, way louder than he should have.

Hoping to preempt an almost certain fight, I maneuvered myself between Titouan and Sam. I shook my head, letting Titouan know he should keep his thoughts to himself, even though I agreed. As I had come to expect, he didn't listen.

"You saw it, and I know damn well you heard what the fuck was happening in that kitchen. Don't pretend you didn't!" Titouan yelled.

"Dammit, Titouan... Lower your voice," I said. Drops of spit flew from my mouth and found their mark in several locations on his face. But a bit of wayward spit was about to seem unimportant.

Several shots rang out. It was hard to tell from exactly where, but if I had to guess, I'd put my money on Barrow High School, which was two or three blocks to the north. While it didn't seem like we were the likely targets for those shots, we were close enough that stray bullets wouldn't have cared whose bodies they destroyed.

There was a small building near the northern side of the runway. I pointed to it and yelled, "Get your asses behind that building!"

More shots rang out as we ran. In my rush towards cover, I was going too fast when I reached the building, lost my balance, and found, to my dismay, that the layer of snow didn't provide nearly as soft of a landing as I would've liked.

"Turn off the lantern," I panted, still trying to catch my breath as I brushed off the snow. "They can't shoot at us if they don't see us." Practicing my own advice, I flipped the off switch on my headlamp.

The building had two doors. At least one of which I hoped would be unlocked. Hope faded to dismay and then gratitude when I saw an open lock hanging from the door. After everyone was safely inside, I decided we had used all our luck on the building being unlocked. "There has to be a way to lock this damn thing," I muttered to myself. I momentarily flicked my lantern on to see what I'd been feeling for. I'll be a sonofabitch, I thought. You could not lock the door from the inside. Not with a lock, anyway. Worse, the door swung inward, as well as outward, meaning it could be pushed in from the outside.

"Anybody have some rope or wire?" No answer.

I fumbled the contents of our hastily packed bags for something I might use to tie the door shut. I couldn't find what I needed, which wasn't completely surprising, given I hadn't thought to pack wire or rope, and I doubted anyone else had, either. With the largest window in our building facing the high school, I didn't want to flip the lantern on again and tempt fate a second time by giving someone an easy shot. I also didn't want someone to casually open the unlocked door and shoot a full magazine of bullets into the building, either. Fate was sending some half-ass doors our way.

I worked my way through the numerous storage bins but wasn't having any luck there, either. I noticed everyone besides Tish and Avery were at least pretending to help. Exactly none of them were looking like their lives might depend on it. At least Titouan was doing his part by keeping an eye on what was happening outside the building. Tish sat on the floor with her knees tucked into her body and hands covering her face. I'd give her a break, too.

Titouan and, maybe, Sam were still in shock because of what happened back at the house. We were safe for the moment, and it seemed like the gunfire had diminished if only slightly. Everyone's nerves were frayed enough without me griping about how lazy they were being.

I'd looked through several bins with no luck when I noticed Avery walking towards me. I stopped, thinking he had something to talk about. I was wrong. He just stopped and stood there. Finally, after several moments, he pulled a small spool of wire out of his pocket. "This wire, while not optimal, should work for this application."

"Thanks," I said. I wasn't sure why I thanked him. He hadn't yet given it to me.

After a couple minutes and a round or two of heated internal debate, he finally handed the spool over to me. He then, without another word, turned and walked away.

I had the wire. I just needed a way to secure the door. On a hope and a prayer, I searched the perimeter of the door for a latching mechanism. Given how the hinges were located on the right side, I assumed if there were a latch, it would be on the opposite side. It wasn't exactly rocket science I was dealing with, which is why I probably guessed right. I found the loop part of the locking system, but there was no hook to secure the door shut with. I would have to figure something else out.

There was a heavy shelf just a couple feet away from the door frame. If it could be slid in front of the door, I could secure the door to it. That would, at the very least, because the door could open outward or inward, keep someone from pulling the door outward. That said, if someone really wanted in, I was willing to bet, even after factoring the heft of the shelf in, they would get in. It wasn't like we were going to stay there. As soon as the shooting died down, we'd be out of there.

After about fifteen minutes, the shelf was in place in front of the door. After another ten, I had wired it as securely as I knew how. Simply put, it was what it was.

***

The building stunk of diesel fuel and grease. Judging from the pieces of equipment inside the building, it was the maintenance department for the airport. It was messy, dark, uncomfortable, and cold; but we seemed to be safe for the moment. The latter, even if mostly psychological, would help keep up the morale of the group.

Looking us over, I saw Tish who was taking things the hardest. I walked over and knelt next to her. "How are you doing?"

"I'm okay," she said, without expression.

"I'm sorry about Tom," I said.

Sam cursed under his breath as Tish said, "Me too."

There was something odd about the way she'd responded. I didn't know if it was the pitch or the tone, or just the cold manner in which the two words had fallen off her tongue. My gaze lingered for a few ticks, but I quickly decided she'd had enough interaction. I needed a break, too. I rolled an old tire to the corner next to the rigged door. Believe it or not, a tire doesn't make a great lounger.

I'd been in my rubber seat for no more than a few seconds when the next hail of gunfire erupted. It lasted several seconds and was punctuated with several individual pops. With the sound ping-ponging off the metal walls, I couldn't tell in which direction the shots had come from.

"Don't seem 'ike 'ey was shootin at us," Sam said.

I half-ass nodded. As long as I didn't hear any bullets plinking off the side of the building, I was content with just resting and shutting my mind off.

Over the next half hour or so, there must've been at least fifty or sixty shots fired. Many of those were quieter, which told me they were further away, at least across the lagoon that separated the two sides of Barrow.

The gunfire abated markedly after that, which allowed us some time for rest and reflection. Sam had fallen asleep but woke because of a nasty nightmare; a shriek and wide eyes let us know he was reliving the day's events. Tish flexed and rubbed her fingers, trying to work feeling back into her near-frozen digits. Avery spent most of that time talking to himself, questioning God, and drawing in the air with his index finger. Titouan just seemed broken. The flimsy exterior that had been created from growing up pampered had crumbled away, leaving behind a huddled mass of a scared twenty-something.

As for me, specifically, I thought about Tom. Irrational as I knew it was, I began doubting my decision to leave him. We had a rifle. Maybe I could've saved him. But, then I set about justifying my decision not to. I thought about what a good guy he was. How strong his character was. He would've wanted us to go. He wouldn't have wanted any of us getting hurt trying to help him. That's just who he was as a man.

But then, you know what I thought? —Fuck that. We say all kinds of crap when we feel guilty. We say things like what my mom told me growing up: "Your dad would've wanted me to remarry. He said he wanted nothing more than for me to be happy. You know that, don't you, William, honey?" In reality, I knew my mom was wrangling longhorns with Earl long before dad died of lung cancer. She told me that crap because she felt guilty for marrying trucker Earl a long two weeks after dad passed away.

"Yeah, Mom, and that Earl... He sure is a good guy. I hope you're happy with him." Actually, I hoped they were enjoying the trailer park they lived in back in Indiana. Ol' Earl got his second OWI and lost his CDL because of it. Soon after the wedding, he'd gotten diabetes and lost a foot. Good thing I can keep a level head about stuff like that. Actually, fuck them, and double-fuck Marlboros. I didn't leave Indiana because I loved my life there.

Irrational tangent aside, or maybe not, I can't read people's minds. For all I knew, Tom might've been thinking, as he chomped on lunch lady, Fat fuck, where the hell are you going? Remember the time I went to the pharmacy to pick up your prescription for the crabs you got off that skanky hooker because you were too embarrassed to do it yourself? The least you could do is go shoot up some of the gray monsters eating the paralyzed chick in the kitchen. Hell, shoot me, so I don't eat her. Go out fighting, you pussy.

The idiotic nature of my thoughts struck me funny, to the point of laughing out loud. All eyes turned to me. Jesus, I felt like I was losing it.

Avery thought my outward showing of madness meant it was time for conversation. He said something, but I was preoccupied trying to think up something that might justify my untimely bout of mirth.

"Huh?" I managed, when I couldn't think up a good excuse.

He looked annoyed, having to repeat himself. "Should we at least talk about what happened?"

Not knowing what to say, I shrugged.

"No one cares what those things are?" He persisted.

He wasn't going to give it a break. Besides, Sam and I needed to clear the air. "Alright, let's talk."

Sam was reading off the same cue card as I was. "Well, son, it's pretty damn simple for me. We just up and left Tom, without carin a fuck 'bout it."

"That wasn't Tom, Sam. And you know it."

"We didn't even try, 'ough. We just left him 'ere ta fend for hisself."

Titouan gave me a look. I shook my head. I then turned to Sam, and in a sullen tone, I said, "I just know that—"

Sam raised both arms and pointed at Titouan and me. "What, you and 'at little sonofabitch over 'ere in cahoots now?"

"Come on. Stop it," I said.

"It's bullshit, what it is—pure damn bullshit."

"Sam," Titouan said.

Oh shit, I thought. Please don't talk, Titouan. Not now.

In a tone that was as controlled and respectful as I had ever heard from him, he finished, "What Tom did back there... wasn't normal. Something happened to him. You have to know that. You have, to," he said, his voice trailing off.

"What Titouan is trying to communicate but is having a tough time saying is, Tom is a cannibal," Avery said, with a slight tremble to his voice.

"God," Tish yelped. I seconded.

"I might be an ignorant ass from Eastern Kentucky, but I done know what happened back 'ere. But 'at don't mean I can't feel like shit for not least tryin." He tugged a few times at his mustache, refusing to make eye contact with anyone during his moment of contemplation. After several absent tugs, he continued, "I heard the same damn thangs you'ins did. I lost a friend—we all did back 'ere—but if what we all seen and heard was real, and I'm pretty damn sure it was, we all lost a hella lot more 'an 'at. Thangs are bad, and we right in the middle of it."

***

My legs were freezing. I got up and walked around, trying to get some blood flow to my lower extremities. I rocked from one foot to the other as I mindlessly took in the surroundings. A few snowflakes floated by as I looked off in the distance. With the full moon and clearing sky, I could see a good distance in three directions. "With all this light, we'll be able to see where we're going."

"That means those things will be able to see us, too," Titouan countered.

"What do we do, then?" I asked. "We can't stay here forever."

"Wait for the authorities to show up and hope whatever those things were back there don't find us."

"Ain't heard a single siren or nothin ta lead me ta think 'ere is any 'thorities. We own our own, fellers," Sam said.

"Somebody is doing a lot of shooting. Who you think is doing that?"

"Lotta guns in Barrow, Tit."

Titouan bristled at being called Tit, but remained calm, for him anyway. "You're talking like the world has just fallen off a cliff. I just don't believe that."

Sam slowly sucked air between his two front teeth and spit before saying, "Funny comin from you... since you was just tellin me 'bout how bad it was back at 'at house."

"You know what I mean, you fuck," Titouan said, sounding more like the petulant Titouan of old.

I cut in. "The point is, we can't defend ourselves in here. If those Grays come looking to do the same thing they did back there at that house, we'll be just as powerless here as we were there. That's just the truth."

"Grays, huh?" Sam asked.

I nodded. I wasn't feeling very imaginative with my naming conventions. They were gray. Why not.

"We're safe here for the moment," Tish said, stone-faced and cold.

I sighed heavily. "For the moment. A moment isn't very long."

Making eye contact this time, and with more vigor, Tish said, "But they're not here now, and they may never find us here. We know they're out there. Why chance it?"

"I say we sleep on it, son. We safe for the time bein."

"Sleep? How in the fuck are we going to sleep in here?" Titouan said.

"Close our damn eyes. How else," Sam said, with a shit-eating grin on his face.

"Anyone besides Titouan disagree?" I asked. When no reply came, I told them, "Let's rest for a little while and decide later."

There were some tarpaulins on a shelf. We spread them on the floor to lie on. They weren't especially comfortable as bedding goes, but they were better than lying directly on the diesel-soaked and grease-stained floor. Normally, stress made me want to sleep, but I was so scared and confused, sleep was the last thing on my mind. It being so cold inside that building only pushed it further away.

They say misery (and self-interest where Titouan was concerned) makes strange bedfellows. It seemed to be true. Instead of sleeping like Sam and Tish, Titouan and Avery were more interested in talking. I drifted in and out of their conversation, spending most of my time glued to the window, and hoping they wouldn't get into another argument. That was until Avery brought up something that tore me from my indifference. He brought up Titouan's ghost.

"I did not exactly tell the truth about what I saw on the ice. I did see a person. His coloration was very similar to the woman back at the house."

Titouan's eyes got wide and a scowl etched at his face. "You made me look like a complete fool, Avery. Why would you not say anything?"

There was a long pause before Avery spoke. "When your nickname is Faux Mulder, no one tends to take what you say very seriously."

"People call me much worse."

Now the two were having a relatable moment. The world was ending.

"I have heard several of them."

Titouan seemed to ignore Avery's comment. "It makes you wonder what he was doing out there alone?"

"My guess is, he was not out there alone. Why would he be? They appear to run in packs."

"Only one attacked Tom," Titouan said.

In the dim light, I saw Avery's head turn toward where I stood next to the window. "I believe there were many in that area. William would attest to that."

Apparently, Avery had heard some of the same strange noises I had. It was quite clear the stigma around his nickname had affected him more than I'd thought. "There sure seemed to be."

Something occurred to me. "Jack said he and Tom had heard the sound of a diesel engine near the Patch. The question is, why would a truck or whatever it was be out there? If what he said was true, and he had no reason to make it up, this opens up a hell of a lot more questions."

There were several moments of silence before Avery spoke up. "What if the truck transported some number of Grays out there?"

Titouan countered. "What if the noise of the truck lured them out there? They seem to be drawn to noise."

Avery nodded. "And smell."

"Lost delivery guy?" Titouan asked.

"I asked Sam about the deliveries. None were due for five days. I doubt very seriously they'd send a truck out in that weather, even if one had been scheduled. I don't think it was that," I said.

"There are several issues here. None of which we know enough about to speculate," Avery said.

I almost laughed aloud at the notion of Avery fearing to speculate. "Never stopped you before."

"If I could come to a logical conclusion about why someone would take those things to the Patch, I would most certainly tell you."

"I'll take a stab at it, then," Titouan said. "If someone brought those things to the Patch, that probably means they have some control over them. If they have control over them, then they probably had something to do with why they are the way they are. There is a military base here in Barrow. Maybe it was an experiment gone wrong. Maybe the military was rounding them up?"

Avery wasn't convinced. "We are talking about genetic alteration on a grand scale."

"It's an Air Force forward-radar base, guys. I'm fairly sure they wouldn't be doing experiments like that there," I said.

"Yeah, and Roswell Airforce Base was only used to teach people how to fly," Titouan said.

Even in the dim light, I could see Avery's eyes grow large with surprise and maybe even approval. "One issue with what you said, Titouan. It is Walker Airforce Base. There was no—"

"I thank I done woke up ta 'nother nightmare. Like I woke up in a damn cold-ass, stinky fuckin room filled with three damned George Norrys. You all might as well go ta sleep. I'll take the watch," Sam said, still lying on his side on the tarp. "'Cause 'is ol' boy ain't goin' back ta sleep."

Of all people, Titouan asked, "What about the Patch?"

"We just got ta hope you nerds are wrong and stick with our plan of goin' ta Miley's," Sam said.

"Miley's is the plan. It always has been. If he's not there, we round up whatever vehicles we can find, and we bust ass back to the Patch and get them," I said.

"And take them where?" Titouan asked.

"All we can take is one step at a time," I said. "We're going to be winging a fair amount of this crap, I'm afraid."

I had just finished my sentence when another round of gunfire erupted. A whole shit load of it, and it was much closer than the previous shots.

"'At's damn close, boys," Sam said.

There was a brief respite in the gunfire followed by shouts in a language none of us understood, from what sounded like a very agitated woman maybe a block away.

Sam and I shared mortified glances before he uttered, "The fuck?"

Thoughts swirled around my mind. Before that, we hadn't seen or heard a fully functional person since arriving in Barrow. For the briefest of moments, I was hopeful. As unlikely as it seemed, maybe this woman was with the Barrow Police or, more unlikely, the military.

Tish, suddenly aroused from her stupor, got up to look out the window. Someone screaming stopped her in her tracks. I waved her back to her seat. She offered no resistance.

Another round of gunfire erupted, near Miley's, followed directly with sounds I couldn't readily identify. The flood of auditory offerings had bottlenecked my ability to fully process what I was hearing. The abject terror I felt didn't exactly foster clarity of thinking, either.

Avery muttered one word: "Grays."

The sound of hundreds of footfalls navigated my bustling auditory system, telling me Avery was right. The materializing silhouettes coming quickly into view completely dashed any remanence of hope I might've had. "Shit," I whispered.

The ghastly procession headed on a crash course that ran parallel with our slapdash shelter. The first two Grays I saw were good runners. They sped past without any hesitation. They were on a mission. What came next was a hodgepodge of Grays. Some walked relatively normal, while most jerked and palsied their way towards the same location the fast runners headed. A couple of them wondered a little too close for comfort, but nothing other than a few hard sniffs in our direction came of it.

That was the case until it wasn't. Something scraped at the side of the building. The corrugated aluminum siding vibrated against my back as whatever-it-was scraped and scratched at it. In concert with the scraping was the sound of feet compacting deep, untrodden snow, mixed with the occasional snort.

I struggled to get my breathing right. I closed my eyes and counted, but that did little to assuage my difficulty. Fuck it, I thought. Go out with a fight. I stood and pressed my face hard against the side of the frosted-over window, trying to get a glimpse of what was making the noise. Then I saw it. A Gray, no more than a few feet from the window, scraped the side of the building with a large butcher knife.

For an instant, I lost control of my ability to stand. I fell at the speed of gravity, my ass again smacking hard concrete. I made way too much noise when my back hit the wall, followed by my head. I managed to stay conscious, but my breathing was in overdrive. The night went quiet.

***

Through the moonlit window, the menacing shadow of the Gray was cast on the ground in front of me. I turned to face the others. Their eyes danced from the window, to me, and then back to the window. No one moved as the scene unfolded outside. The curious Gray decided something was special about the building. He seemed determined to explore it, one way or another.

I heard what I thought was the sound of plastic wrap being crinkled. Then I realized it was the sound of a flexing pane of glass above me. The windowpane began spider-webbing as the Gray applied increased pressure. There was a brief silence before the window exploded inward, shards of glass shot across the inside of the building and on my head and shoulders.

He stuck his head in, sniffed, and grunted. Avery whimpered loudly. Sam grabbed his face and pulled it close to his. "Be quiet, boy," he hissed. The Gray snorted hard in Sam and Avery's direction, slamming something into the side of the building as he removed his head from inside.

Sam released Avery's head and slowly moved towards the rifle against the wall.

I grew dizzy from the rapidity of my shallow pants. I needed to control my breathing.

Once the Gray decided he couldn't get in through the window, he began to move away. Momentarily, I thought he'd left. He was eerily quiet. The respite of silence ended when the scraping started anew. This time on the eastern side of the building. He was walking around the damn building.

Titouan panicked. "What do we do? What do we do? What do we do?" He repeated.

"Shut up, damn you," Sam said, in what couldn't be misconstrued as a whisper.

The scraping sound neared the still-locked entrance. With a thud, the Gray threw his weight into it: once, twice, and three times before quitting. Avery repeated something under his breath. A prayer. At least he was whispering during his mental breakdown.

I'd managed not to pass out. I was in semi-control of my breathing.

The scraping terminated at the door. A long pause ensued—way too long of a pause. The shelf then shook as the Gray pushed the door. Another pause. He pushed again; this time, the shelf slid a good foot, allowing the door to open enough we were blasted with cold air.

The Gray sniffed but then went quiet. For a moment, I hoped he might move along, but was quickly reminded that hope was something that should be set aside for a sunnier day. Without warning, the Gray smashed through the door. The so-called heavy shelf toppled first, followed directly by the door—which couldn't have been attached to the wall by more than scotch tape and a Band-Aid—which the Gray rode to the ground in a crash. He bounced up, sniffed, and ran headlong towards Sam.

"Shoot him, dammit," I managed.

Click.

"Oh shit, son," was all Sam could get out before the Gray was on him.

Sam held the Gray at bay with the gun between them. The Gray snapped his teeth and flailed the knife wildly and, luckily for Sam, inaccurately. Sam grunted as he pitched the Gray to his left. He was free of the attacker, but Avery gained one, thanks to his proximity to Sam during the attack.

Tish fled to the other side of the building, not bothering to help.

I saw Sam try to grab the Gray, but he was stabbed in the leg for his effort. He fell backward in pain. I then decided to help, but the man was too powerful. I ended up on my ass for the effort.

"He is biting me!" Avery screamed. He followed that with cries of being forsaken.

Instantly, I thought about loitering Grays. If they heard him scream, they would soon join in with the one who was already attacking us. We could barely handle him. Shit. I grabbed hold of the Gray as Sam pounded him with the butt of the rifle. The Gray swung the knife wildly, somehow missing everyone while sinking his teeth into what looked like Avery's hand. My near stroking-out due to hyperventilation for the ten minutes prior had rendered me near useless.

Titouan came up behind the Gray. With Tish's knife in hand, he stabbed the Gray repeatedly until he fell lifeless on top of Avery. I fell to the side, struggling for every breath. I saw Tish sitting in the corner. "Get over here, Tish," I yelled between pants.

She was frozen. "Dammit, Tish... we need you.... Sam's cut... and Avery's bit."

"My hand. He bit my hand. I am bleeding," Avery said.

"That bastard got me good," Sam said, grimacing and trying to hold pressure on his cut while also taking a look at Avery's hand.

"Tish!" I yelled.

Titouan was looking in Tish's bag for something. "What are you doing!" I asked.

"Bandages," he huffed.

He ran the bandage over to me. "Thanks, Titouan," I said as I tore off a decent length, which I used to hastily wrap Avery's hand with. Tish was going to have to work on Sam's.

I looked over at Sam. "How you doing over there?"

"Bleedin like a stuck pig."

Tish crouched next to him. About damn time, I thought.

"You okay, bud?"

"Perhaps," he said, his eyelids clamped tight, while holding his hand out for my inspection.

I looked it over for a second. It seemed like a superficial wound to me. He proffered an aggrieved whimper as I switched my attention to Sam, who seemed to be have gotten the worst end of the attack. "How bad is it?" I asked Tish.

She didn't offer an immediate reply. My frustration mounted with each second that passed without her saying anything. I thought about asking her again but wasn't sure I could control my temper. Believing my attention would be better served mending the busted door, I began in that direction. I had taken a single step when Tish said, very succinctly, "It'll need stitches." Without turning towards her, I replied, in an equally succinct manner. "Okay."

After the door was even more half-ass in-place, I grabbed one of the tarps we were using as bedding and into roughly the size to cover the window. It would also work as a barrier against the cold, blasting wind.

I spied some rebar on the floor. I leaned a few of the heavy rods against the sides of the tarp to hold it up for a moment. I then ran over to my backpack and grabbed the one thing I was very thankful I'd brought: duct tape. I went about using most of the roll to seal the tarp to the wall. I left the rebar in place as an extra precaution because of the high winds. The good news was the window was covered, and we could turn our lamps on. The bad news was we no longer had a window to look out of.

Avery didn't look well. He sat with his back against the wall, holding his bandaged hand and staring at the thing lying dead on the floor. "Are you okay?" I asked.

Never taking his eyes off the Gray, he said, "Am I going to turn into that?"

"No," I said. I meant, I didn't think he would.

Chapter 7

I had just finished filling a kerosene heater when I heard a commotion near the rear entrance of the Commons. I quickly screwed the lid back on the jug and ran to the back to see what was going on. The lady doing the yelling, our cook, Olivia Danmar, was visibly shaking. In between long breaths, she said, "I'm telling you what I saw, Jim. Somebody's outside."

"Of course, somebody's outside. Probably more than one. It smells like smoke and ass in here," Jim said.

"What's going on?" I asked.

"I saw someone. Didn't you hear me say that?"

"Well, yeah, but as Jim said, people need to get some fresh air every now and again."

By the sour look on her face, I could tell she thought I wasn't taking her seriously. "How about you catch your breath and start from the beginning."

She shook her head angrily as she worked on her breaths. "Well, some of it's personal."

Confused, I said, "Uh... okay. What's personal?"

She whispered, "With the power being out, and it being dark and all, I left in a hurry this morning, forgetting things a decent woman shouldn't ever forget." She peered down at her, uh, ample, but also gravity-affected, bosom before also tracing the outline of her nether region with her index finger, to indicate she'd forgotten to wear a certain other garment. The mental image was cringeworthy. I needed to make it all stop.

"How about just the part that's got you so upset?"

She nervously ran her fingers over her bluish-gray coif of hair. "I saw a man without a coat over by the Nest."

"Who was it?"

Her eyes darted between me and Jim before finally settling on me. "I don't know."

"What do you mean, you don't know? Everybody knows everybody."

"Because he doesn't work on the Patch. If you all would let me finish, I'd tell you these things," she said, her hands firmly planted on her hips.

I put my hands up in submission. "Sorry."

She took a couple calming breaths before continuing, "I never saw him in my life." She paused.

"I believe you. Just continue," I said.

"I was about to ask him if he was okay, you know, because he wasn't wearing a coat and all, but before I could, he turned towards me, and the damn fool started spinning like a top. Like a top." She got a little closer to Jim and me like she knew a secret and didn't want anyone else to know. "He was all hopped-up on drugs, I bet."

If you wanted the down-low of what was happening at the Patch, gossip-wise, Olivia was your woman. Right down to the seedy details. Because of that, I was reluctant to act. But she of all people should've at least known who the dude was. I couldn't take any chances. There were too many weird things happening for me to be too dismissive. "Jim, close and lock all the doors in the commons, and a couple of us are going to have to check this dude out."

Jim shot me an odd look. He began to say something but settled instead on a quick rolling of his eyes. Olivia shot him a look. Finally, Jim threw up his hands and said, "You're the boss." I wasn't sure whether he was talking to me or Olivia. Either way, he did as he was asked.

As for Olivia, I put my hands on her shoulders and told her to go rest and that we would make sure everyone was safe. She began to say something, but I told her to, "Go on now."

She wouldn't budge.

"What?"

"You all need to be careful. You know all the crazy drugs people take in Barrow. He might have super-human strength."

"Thanks, Olivia... I'll keep that in mind."

She'd taken ten steps before she'd cornered someone else, telling him no-doubt about her harrowing experience outside.

"Well, I am being wery sorry about your experience," the man said.

Stifling a laugh, I decided to interrupt their conversation, saving him from it, "Hey, Aadesh," I called out. "I need you to come here for a minute."

After issuing a quick apology, he practically ran to me. Olivia glared at me before stomping off. The Commons was a captive audience. She'd find someone else to ear-rape. I was sure of that.

"I am wery appreciative of you saving me from dad woman. She is windy."

"Well, don't thank me much. I need you to check the drill shack."

He looked concerned. "I came from dere. Id was empdy."

"Well, I need you to go back. You heard what she said. Someone could be out there."

"I did see him, Jack!" Olivia yelled from across the Commons.

"Poor word choice, Olivia. My bad," I called back, wondering how in the hell she'd heard what I said.

A crowd of people began gathering around Aadesh and me, trying to find out what the newest source of turmoil was. "Anyway, just go back over there and check. I'd hate for you to have to explain to Titouan how things were stolen."

"Yes, I do nod wand to be delling him dad. Bud I am nod wery crazy aboud going oud dere being dad a crazy man being on the lam."

"Take the rifle, then. Just don't shoot anybody."

The offer seemed to have taken him by surprise. "You are asking me do dake de weapon? I have only fired id once, and id was nod wery successful. Sam wanded do bead me aboud my head wid id afder I discharged id premadurely."

"Just be careful with it. And don't prematurely fire it. I'm sure you won't need to fire it at all."

"Doors are locked," Jim said as he nudged his way through the people who had encircled us.

"Well, Aadesh and I are going outside. Lock them behind us. Don't let anyone inside."

Jim chuckled. "You really are letting Aadesh take the rifle?"

I shrugged. "Yeah... why not?"

"He doesn't know how to shoot it."

"I know."

"I can go out with him, or wake up some of the other guys..."

"Nah." I looked towards Olivia, who was neck-deep in her retelling to some poor shmuck who happened to be in the wrong place at the wrong time. "I think things will be okay."

"If you say so. I'll have someone watch the other door for Aadesh. I'll wait for you at the main entrance."

I patted him on the back. "Thanks."

Jim locked the door behind me. I didn't bother turning my lamp on. It was twilight, and the snow was starting to let up. It sounds weird, but I felt safer with the light out. I pulled my hood over my head and walked quickly over to the lean-to, which seemed like a good starting point. That, and a quick sip of tequila, sounded good.

The only thing of interest in the lean-to was the mostly empty bottle of Sam's tequila. "Drink 'at Tequiler, shit, and you won't even need no heat," Sam had told us earlier that night. I was feeling a nice chill about then. I thought I would take ol' boy's advice. A couple swigs later, the bottle was finished. Sam knew his shit. I was feeling warmer.

I let the alcohol run its course. After all that we had been through over the last several hours, I needed it. That's when it hit me like a brick, and I'm not talking about the alcohol, either. I had failed to link what had happened earlier with Tom and me with what Olivia had seen. I needed to have been taking things much more seriously than I was, but that was a long-standing problem with me. As I often did, I vowed to do better. I tipped the empty bottle one more time, savoring the last couple drops, before leaving the building.

I was getting ready to latch the lean-to door closed when someone slammed into me, nearly knocking me to the ground in the process. "Are you blind, bro," I asked, startled, but mostly joking.

His face was awash with wide-eyed surprise. "Hey, who are you?" I asked.

The first thing I noticed, besides his wide eyes and a menacing brow, was the rifle he had slung on his shoulder. "What are you doing here? Are you the police?" I asked.

He didn't reply. Instead, he began unslinging his rifle; and, considering how he looked at me, I knew I was in trouble. As he brought the rifle up to what I assumed was a firing position, I slung my lantern around as fast as I could and I struck him hard in the face. I then jumped on the bastard. He dropped his gun—looked like a machine gun to me, but I was from a part of California where it was uncool to have a gun, much less know anything about them.

I grabbed the gun and was on my feet in one quick motion. I aimed the barrel between his eyes. "Who the hell are you? If you're the police, this is on you, man." Shots rang out somewhere near the Commons, followed by what sounded like hundreds of feet slamming into the snow. "Dude, if you don't fucking talk right now, I'm going to do something bad to you. I mean it," I said, taking another quick look at the Commons.

Feeling completely vulnerable, I told him, "Get up and get in the building, now." He lay back and sneered at me. I put the point of the rifle barrel into his left cheek and pushed hard. "Look at me, asshole," I told him. There was chaos at the Commons by that time, and I needed to be over there, but I couldn't leave this guy. "Last time, get inside now!"

His eyes were locked with mine, the look of hate was slathered all over his face.

"Dude, if you don't move in about two seconds, we're going to have a problem."

I noticed his hand slowly moving towards his pocket, retrieving a black box. He grasped it with both hands and began to turn a knob. POP! He screamed in agony as he dropped whatever was in his hand and clutched his mangled face. I pulled the trigger. I meant to, I guess. I didn't have a choice, I thought. But...

"Oh, my God... oh, my God," I said. "You didn't talk to me... You didn't listen to me, dude! It's your fault... I didn't want to do it. I didn't want to blow your fucking face off," I said, panicking. "Dammit, you asshole!"

The man tried to say something, but I couldn't understand him. "Now you try to talk, damn you!"

I heard shouts in a language I didn't understand. It sounded like Japanese. I then saw people walking slowly towards where they thought the shot came from. The Commons was fully enveloped in chaos.

I had my own problems, though. The people walking towards me had to have noticed me by that point. I tore myself away from what was happening at the Commons and in the process of gathering my senses also gathered up the man's belongings, plus my own. I ran back outside.

I paced for a moment. "What the hell am I going to do?" I asked myself. "I just shot that dude. Damnit!" My contemplation of previous events would have to wait. There were footsteps and light conversation close enough for me to hear.

The only thing I could think of was to hide. I had the gun, but if it hadn't fired when I... Well, I would've been completely screwed. I wasn't going to rely on it a second time. A split second later, I was feeling the cold sidewall of the lean-to, between the exit and the bathroom. My hands probed the small raised part of the corrugated aluminum. "There you are," I said quietly. I moved the piece of aluminum just enough so that there was a gap large enough for me to squeeze through. I then slid the aluminum door back into to place.

When we'd heard Titouan was taking over at the Patch, we knew he'd put a stop to us smoking weed. So, like any good group of potheads, we'd improvised. There was a light fixture on the sidewall, and Sam had requisitioned from Avery a super-powerful fan that vented the smoke so no one close to the lean-to could smell it. It had worked perfectly. Now, I hoped it would function half as well as a hiding spot for me.

At least two people were outside the lean-to, talking to the man I'd shot. I didn't understand what they were saying, but it was clear the woman questioning him wasn't happy. The man's whimpering turned to crying. It didn't matter that I didn't know what was being said; the language of begging was universal. His cries became muffled. Smothered, I thought. Within moments, there was only silence.

They moved slowly and methodically into the lean-to. I could barely hear them over the wind, but I felt the vibrations from the sidewall as they passed through the entrance. At some point, they no longer tried to mask themselves.

A woman yelled out to me in perfect English, "We're here to help."

Yeah, fuck you all, I thought. Either they thought I was deaf or stupid, because I could hear what was happening over at the Commons. The bastards were not there to help.

"We know you're in here," came a third voice.

The woman spoke several curt words in whatever language they spoke, apparently not directed at me. There was a squawk from a radio, followed by a quick and efficient reply. Then, there was nothing but silence for what seemed like a solid five minutes. I was sweating it bad. My entire body shook.

I had a lot of other things on my mind, like not dying, but there was a terrible smell coming from somewhere. It filled the lean-to. I sniffed my coat sleeve. I fought back a gag. My sleeve had this nasty, mucusy film covering it. It was so bad, I feared they might smell it through the wall.

There were two quick shots into what I thought was the bathroom, then the mirror fell to the ground with a crash. The bathroom door flung open hard; the sound it made when it slammed against the fake wall of the dope room sounded hollower than it should have because there was no actual framing behind the fake wall, just a thick sheet of corrugated aluminum.

I heard what sounded like hundreds of footsteps coming from the direction of what I thought was the Commons. There was another shot fired into the bathroom. Sensing that there were going to be more shots fired, I slowly got down on my belly. I figured the racket being made outside would obscure any noise I might've made moving to the floor. Like clockwork, someone opened fire all along the wall of the bathroom and dope room. I could see the rays of lamplight now shining through the newly created holes in the wall.

The sounds that replaced the gunfire were nightmarish. It will suffice to say that what I heard didn't sound human, not to me anyway. There was sniffing and snorting with the occasional grunt thrown in for atmosphere. I shook even more violently.

"Friend, if you're in there, we'll find you," the woman said, now outside the building. The sniffs and snorts ramped up as she spoke. I heard a disturbance outside, followed by the sickening sound of a bone-crushing blow from something heavy. Something or someone fell to the ground with a thud. She then picked back up the conversation like nothing had happened. "If you're in there, you'll want to let me know. You don't want those terrible things you hear to find you. I'll make it quick and painless. They won't," she said, with a hint of glee in her voice.

At least she was honest.

The radio squawked again. "I'll be right there—" the woman started in English, then caught herself and switched to the other language. The woman then barked orders to those who were with her. There was the ping of a couple metal objects hitting the floor, followed by the Sniffers becoming highly agitated.

The lantern light diminished as the woman and her human entourage moved away. Regrettably, the Sniffers and their nightmare-inducing bellows remained.

In just a matter of moments, I heard what sounded like bodies violently jostling one another maybe thirty feet from the lean-to. Thanks to the light from the multiple lanterns having been set up around the spectacle and a favorable bullet hole, I had a front-row seat to the unfolding events.

Several people from the Patch were made to get down on their knees. Sobbing and begging filled the dark night. One man spoke up, uttering a single word: "Why?" A man walked up to him and, without hesitation, slammed the butt of his rifle into the man's gut. His name was John. He was one hell of a cook. He fell over on his side and was still for several moments before finally sucking in a long breath.

The woman walked slowly around those who were made to kneel. The large, furred hood she wore obscured her face, but that voice of hers she called out with was clear. "I'm going to begin killing your friends, if you don't come out now. This is your only warning," the woman yelled.

If I'm being honest, up until that point in my life, I had pretty much shirked away from any and all responsibilities. I left my mom and dad's business because they'd expected too much from me. I was too chill to be a suit-and-tie guy, anyway. I wanted to live on my own terms, not be a snotty suit-wearing shill who sipped wine and talked about bullshit that didn't amount to anything. I moved to Texas and got hooked up with Miley and William. I got to see the world, do cool things, and got my fingernails dirty. All the while, by doing whatever the hell I wanted.

One way or another, I guess, things end up coming full circle. The yen and yang of life. My shirking days were over. I had to make a decision and live with it. Granted, this decision had a hell of a lot more hanging in the balance than balance sheets and hobnobbing with other knob-gobblers.

I had to know what they wanted. In my mind, the contents of the bag I'd taken had to be important as hell for them to be willing to execute people for. I quietly unzipped the dead man's bag; a few clips for the rifle in there, several small, metallic cube-looking things, three or four tubes of what looked like toothpaste, but I was sure wasn't, and a weird black box.

I jumped as the leader began to talk again. "Apparently, you think you can keep our property without consequences. You can't." There was a loud pop, and a thud from a body falling over. There were screams and loud crying. Some of the Sniffers who were outside the lean-to took off running towards the shots. Several more shots rang out, and more bodies fell to the ground.

"Let's try this again. You have one minute, and then I'm going to shoot two of your friends."

Part of me wanted it all over. I wanted to just run over there and give them the bag. I knew what would happen, though. They would've killed me, gotten their bag back, and then they would've killed everyone on the Patch. You didn't smother the life out of one of your own if you didn't mean business. I couldn't. I knew what was going to happen. But those bastards were going to pay for what they did to my friends. Not then, but they would later.

She kept her word. There were two quick pops followed by, well, you know—followed by more Sniffers running towards the shooting, followed by them also being mowed down. Tears ran down my face. I don't know why I did what I did, but I punched myself in the jaw. I needed to feel something, but I was numb. I was letting people die, but I didn't have a choice.

"What is your name?"

"Oliv... Olivia," she said, crying.

"You think you know who has my things?"

"Yes..." She said. "It's either— It's either Jack, or Aadesh. They were the only ones outside the Commons... when you people showed up."

"Tell them how afraid you are."

Olivia pleaded with us to bring them their things. That's probably all needs to be said. She can't be held accountable for all of what she was forced to say.

"If they haven't brought me my things by the time you count to thirty, I am going to kill you. Okay?"

"No... please," Olivia begged.

"Count!"

Olivia reached thirty. The woman was good for her word. She shot Olivia. I fell to the floor, unable to watch any longer.

I don't remember much after that. There was yelling, and more gunshots. There might've even been more executions. I didn't really think about anything else. I just remember staring into the darkness. There wasn't much effort needed for that. Just look. Accept it. Move on.

I settled into a quiet meditation. In it all, I lost track of time. An hour might've passed. It could've been a week, for all I knew. I just remember things being quiet after a time. No snorts, sniffs, cries, or other things fortunate people never hear. Just me and the dark silence of being alone.

***

Snapping to attention, I heard footsteps outside the lean-to. Quiet footsteps. They were the kind of steps someone took when hiding from something. The footsteps stopped directly in front of me. I heard fingers probing the same places mine had earlier. Someone knew about the fake wall. Maybe someone told them about it. I slowly raised the gun to fire.

The door slid open. "Don't move," I said.

"Shid, man!"

I knew instantly who it was. Shit. "Aadesh, I almost killed you."

"If I knew how do shood dis damn ding, I would have dried do kill you also," he said.

"Get in here."

"Everyone is dead. Id is derrible oud dere... all our dead friends," he said, his hands clasped to the sides of his head as he walked in circles in the small space.

"We should probably be quiet." I paused for a moment. "But I'm glad you're alive, too, Aadesh."

"I believe dey have all lefd the premises. I heard wehicles being sdarded and dem moving away wery quickly. I am nod sure do where, dough."

"I didn't hear any of that... I just... What are you doing, man?"

He popped open the wooden box we kept the weed in and retrieved a roach, which he then lit up. "I am glad no one finished dis."

"Put it out," I yelled. "The sniffers will smell it... and we'll—"

"Chill, bro. I'll pud id oud," Aadesh said, after taking two long hits before throwing it to the ground and stomping on it.

After several moments of awkward silence, he was ready to talk again. I wasn't. "Dey killed eweryone bud us..." his voice shook, and I thought he might cry.

"Aadesh, bro... I can't talk about this right now, okay?"

He coughed and spat. "I am sorry. Bud id is horrible, Jack— wery horrible. Why would dey do dis?"

"I don't know."

"Jim tried to hide in the drill shack..." He stopped.

I looked at him. "Please, dude, stop."

"Okay. I am being manic. I know dis."

Aadesh had a terrible chemical smell to him that was making me sick and dizzy. "Dude, you're flammable. I can't believe you lit that joint."

"Our friends were murdered. My brain is nod working wery well ad de momend."

I deflected away from our friends. I asked a question I already knew the answer to. "Did you hide in the mud pits?"

Some of his nervous energy was beginning to wear off. The drag or two off the roach probably was having an effect, too. "Yes," he said, much less animated than before.

He was soaked and freezing and needed to get dry and warm very soon or things were going to be very bad for him. Until that point, I hadn't even realized how much I was shaking. "I'll go to the supply room in the Commons. That's where the kerosene is. We'll get warm and figure out our next move. Are you sure they're gone?"

"I heard a woman yelling at someone on a phone or radio or someding. I did nod know whad dey were saying, bud dey were raising dere voices wid one anoder. Id was after dad when dey lefd de premises. Dey lefd wery quickly and were nod happy do have done so."

"There are some blankets on Sam's cot. Wrap yourself up, and I'll be back as quickly as I can with the kerosene."

"Is dad a good idea?"

"We'll find out, won't we?

Shivering, he said, "Okay."

***

On the way over to the Commons, I made sure to give the area where I thought Olivia and the others had been executed a wide berth, but there was no way of escaping the carnage. At least ten bodies scattered the floor not thirty yards from the lean-to. One of them was face down in the snow, with his rear end sticking up. I didn't see Olivia, but I knew she was there.

Upon entering, I was greeted with just enough light from the two still burning kerosene heaters to see the shadowy forms making up the macabre scene inside. Bodies were everywhere, all of which were lying in one life-snuffed-out pose or another. Near the supply room, which I'd locked to keep people from getting at the kerosene, lay a clump of bodies just outside. As I fumbled trying to find the correct key, I refused to think about why there were so many bodies just outside the door. I knew, of course, they were almost certainly trying to hide in the supply room, but I didn't let myself dwell on it at the time. I would do enough dwelling later.

I quickly hand-pumped enough kerosene to fill the small container and was on my way back to the lean-to when I heard what I was sure was moaning to my left. In a room full of stillness, you notice movement; a man stirred just a few feet away. I turned the lamp to its lowest setting and moved cautiously to where he was lying. I didn't recognize him, and instantly regretted not bringing the rifle. "Who are you?" I asked.

He began to speak but stopped, grabbed his stomach, and coughed mucous all over himself and me. After the coughing had subsided, he began to speak, but I couldn't understand what he was saying. After another fit of coughing he spoke again. This time in English. "I couldn't do it," he said, repeatedly.

"Couldn't do what?"

"I couldn't kill for the Order."

"Look, I don't know what you're talking about, bro. What the hell is the Order?"

"You have to leave. I'm going to turn... They, made me drink it." He began coughing again.

"I don't understand—"

"You have to go. Now!" he yelled. "Don't you understand?" he began to sob, "I'm going to turn."

"Why... Why did you have to kill my friends?"

Before he could say anything, he began to retch. The back of his head pounded the floor in sickening, fleshy thuds. A geyser of vomit erupted from his mouth. He began to choke on his own rancid liquids. I tried to turn his head, but it was locked in place, his muscles so tight the skin on his neck was pulled up in tight furrows. Not knowing what else to do, I pulled him to his side, hoping to keep him from choking to death. The choking stopped, but for whatever reason, he still couldn't breathe.

I let him fall to his back. His head pointed towards the ceiling, but his terrified eyes sought mine as he gasped for air that wouldn't come. His face began to turn an odd shade of gray. Don't die, I thought. I needed answers. And then he went still. His terrified eyes closed. His body seemed to relax.

I moved closer, trying to hear any signs of breathing. My face was mere inches from his when his eyes jerked open. The lack of oxygen seemed to have damaged them. They were terrible to look at; gray and lifeless. I yelped as his hand grabbed my hood and pulled me so close I could feel (and smell) whiffs of breath carrying inaudible rasps of unformed words. I fought to get away, but his grip wouldn't give. He was trying to tell me something. "Don't drink... water... Ruuun," he finally managed, before going completely still and lifeless.

The Commons fell eerily silent. I could hear and feel my heart beating out of my chest. For me, in that dreadful instant, there was a reckoning; not only had my friends been brutally murdered for a reason I couldn't explain, something else much more ominous loomed in the cold darkness of that night. Something seemingly unexplainable yet obvious occurred to me. Someone had attacked us using the sniffing things as weapons.

Sniffing things, I thought. They were not things, or at least hadn't been, formerly. They had been average Joes like me. Then, though, they'd been reduced to monsters. My thoughts began to drift towards the whys and hows, but I didn't allow it. There was no time for that.

I shivered as I took one last glance at the man who had created more questions than answers. I grabbed my things and began walking towards the lean-to.

When I entered, Aadesh was pacing feverishly. "Jesus, man, I did nod dink you were coming back."

"Sorry." I began trying to pour the kerosene into the heater, but my hands were shaking so badly most of it ended up on the floor.

"Whad is wrong," Aadesh said, his teeth chattering.

I looked at him like, dude, really? I then pushed the igniter button on the heater. There was a poof sound, then glorious heat filled the room as I cranked the heater up to full blast. Something felt good, at least.

"Jack?"

I showed him my shaking hands. "It's bad."

Aadesh nodded.

"One of the attackers was still alive."

"Did you have do—?"

"No. I think they poisoned him. Apparently, he didn't have the stomach for killing our people."

"Doo bad de others did."

"We have to leave."

"We do nod have a wehicle."

I nodded. "The problem isn't leaving. I have an idea for that. The problem is finding where we need to go."

Aadesh walked over to one of the delivery bays and pointed. "We know in which direcdion Barrow lies. If we direcd ourselves on the course in which I currendly poind, we will come upon Barrow or some close vicinidy dereof."

"Yeah, but how do we stay on the correct heading?"

"I do nod know eweryding. I know dis is" —again pointing with his index finger— "roughly de correcd heading. Dad is all I know, okay?"

"We have no choice. After we warm-up for a bit, we'll go see if there's any juice in the battery Avery used to fire up the heater. If there is, we'll try to take the front-end loader."

"De one dad is used to clean dis facilidy of snow?"

"Yes."

"I believe id only has seading for one?"

"We'll put you in the bucket." He looked at me skeptically. "Do you know how to drive it?"

"No. Bud I'm nod sure I wand do ride in de bucked. Id is really cold."

"Well, there is always walking?"

"I'll ride in de bucked."

***

We went about the task of getting everything together we thought we needed, including the ten blankets Aadesh believed necessary for him to not freeze to death. Whatever, I thought. If that kept him from griping, and we could fit the other things in there, he could take whatever he thought he needed.

I had the battery in the loader and was ready to try it. The lights switched on. That was a good sign. I turned the key, and a plume of smoke came out of the stack as it came to life on the first try. "I'll be damned," I said out loud, "the damn thing runs!" Aadesh gave me the thumbs up, and he began to quickly load things into the bucket. I had the rifle and the bag I'd taken from the man, plus a few odds-and-ends, in the cab with me. Everything else, including Aadesh's rifle, was with him.

I oriented the bucket a few feet off the ground and in such a manner that he could lie down without worrying about rolling out. I did a quick check of my gear in the cab and was getting ready to put the front-end loader in gear when I saw someone moving towards the driver's door. I was getting ready to let Aadesh know how stupid it was to get out of the bucket without letting me know, when I noticed it wasn't Aadesh.

Instead, it was the guy I found sick in the Commons, except he didn't seem sick anymore—not exactly, anyway. His head jerked crazily as he came closer and closer to the cab. "Fuck this," I said aloud while closing the door.

Without warning, the guy tried getting to me in the cab. Luckily for me, he wasn't coordinated enough to climb the three steps necessary to access the door, or smart enough to reach for the door handle that was easily within reach of his grasping hands. All he could manage to do was pound with his fists on the bottom of the door.

I switched the loader into gear and goosed the gas. We lurched forward. I saw Aadesh now standing up in the bucket and pointing ahead of us. His eyes were wide with fear. I pointed to the guy pounding on the cab door. He waved and pointed frantically ahead, ignoring the bigger problem I was dealing with. I put my hands in the air, letting him know I didn't have a clue what he was talking about. Then I saw exactly what he was talking about.

Through the powerful lights of the loader, I could see figures emerging from the dark. First one, and then two, three... I lost count at ten. The leading edge of the group was almost on Aadesh, and he was making sure I knew how bad of a predicament he was in. He also made sure to let me know, with animated gestures, that he wanted to get the hell out of the bucket. I yelled, "Stay in the fucking bucket!" I then raised it up several feet in the air, out of their reach. His wide eyes relaxed, albeit only slightly.

I don't know why, but I tried to reason with the dude pounding on the cab door. "Get the hell away," I said, gesticulating that he should move away from the rear wheel that was coming very close to squishing him. His big, black eyes focused contently on mine until he lost his balance or just couldn't keep up anymore. His body was a scant hindrance to the big wheels as he passed under.

I turned my attention to the other attackers, while also slowly increasing the speed of the loader. One of them was quick fodder for the front left wheel. Another spun in circles, confused about what he should be doing. Some of the others were simply too slow to react to the loader as we sped by. There were two of them, though, who managed to time things correctly and jump on both the right and left front fenders, in something that seemed too coordinated for my liking.

The one on my left was especially adept. In a couple motions, he hopped on the foot peg and then quickly bounded off it and squarely onto a perch on the fender. The one on my right, although in a much less agile manner, grasped the fender and willed himself up.

I remember their gray faces vividly. There was evil intent in their eyes. While they didn't exactly look inhuman, they were different enough. I wasn't going to be too upset if they, too, found themselves under the big wheels of the loader. Especially since the one on the left was trying his damnedest to climb the bucket arm to get to Aadesh.

I pantomimed that Aadesh should use the gun to shoot the nearest Sniffer. He looked confused. The idea of using the gun to shoot someone seemed to hit home hard. He fumbled with the rifle. The other Sniffer was stuck on the fender, not sure of what he should do next. We would concentrate on the other one first, assuming Aadesh didn't shoot himself in the process.

With one hand on the control throttle, and the left side of my right foot pressing down on the seat so the safety switch wouldn't cut the engine, I opened the cab door and yelled out to Aadesh. "Shoot him, dammit!"

The Sniffer looked at Aadesh, then back at me before settling on the closest target, Aadesh. He went back to trying to find a way to get him.

At least by that point, Aadesh was holding the rifle in a firing position. The gray was close enough that he could just put the tip of the barrel on the Sniffer's head and fire. He got part of that correct. He used the tip of the barrel to poke the Sniffer. Except that he couldn't put enough force behind it to dislodge him from the arm.

"Shoot him!" I yelled.

Finally, a shot was fired, and the Sniffer fell to the ground. Aadesh had shot him in what looked like his neck. Wherever he hit him, he was now off the loader. Aadesh, looking very pale, ejected a vomitus spray, followed by a long string of words I wasn't sure made any sense at all. Besides, I was still worried about the Sniffer still on the fender riding out the rough terrain.

I serpentined the loader, trying to fling him off, but he was holding on for dear life. With all my attention being paid to the hitchhikers, I hadn't noticed the lights approaching quickly from behind us. Aadesh's eyes got wide again. He saw the truck speeding to my left, going way faster than it should have been on the ice. The window was down, and the man had a gun aimed in our direction.

Luckily for us, the truck slammed into a large snowbank, causing the shots to harmlessly whizz over our heads. The big diesel momentarily lost control. Somehow, the driver managed to pull it back from the brink just in time to dodge a larger snowdrift that very well could've incapacitated the vehicle. In a matter of moments, they were back in the chase and positioning for another pass.

To Aadesh's credit, he had his rifle up and ready to fire. I was preparing to shoot mine as well. I kept my foot on the gas, while I let the loader go wherever its misaligned steering took it, leaving my hands free to fire my weapon.

The truck was dangerously close. Aadesh held the rifle close to his face, trying to line a shot up with the scope. He fired once and fell back into what I hoped was the bucket. I didn't see him fall to the ground, and I didn't think he was shot. I just knew I didn't see him. The guy in the truck fired several shots, most of which pinged off the bucket or the bucket arms.

At that same time, I had my gun aimed at the door of the man firing at Aadesh. They didn't seem to think I was a threat, or maybe they didn't see that I was also armed. I pulled the trigger, but nothing happened. "What the shit," I yelled, panicking. I couldn't figure out how to make the damn thing work, and the darkness of the cab made it nearly impossible to see. I cried out in anger. The shooter was now firing unchallenged towards us.

The only thing that kept me alive was the rough ice on which the big truck traveled. It had to make shooting difficult at best. With enough shots, bad terrain or not, a lucky shot was going to find its mark. It was really only a matter of time.

Movement in the bucket pulled my attention away from our pursuers. The rifle was resting on the top edge of the bucket, and it looked like Aadesh was having another go at returning fire. I saw a flash from the muzzle and then another. I thought to myself that he had about six or seven shots before we die. More shots were fired in our direction, one of which hit the steering wheel. A searing pain engulfed me, and I felt something wet flowing down my neck and chest. A damn bullet had nicked my chin.

I veered the loader to the right, trying to get out of the line of fire. Apparently, my swerving had allowed Aadesh to fire a perfect shot. Or, depending on how you looked at it, a lucky shot. He fired five shots in the truck's direction. I then swerved hard to the left and disappeared into the night. "Holy shit!"

Aadesh stood in the bucket, firing at least two more shots in the direction of the truck that had, by then, veered severely away from us. He pointed in the direction I last saw the truck and mimed that he'd seen it crash through the ice. I then decreased the loader's speed and swung in the opposite direction. Whether they were going too fast, or they had just hit a bad patch of ice—either way, they were gone, and we were safe for the moment.

After several more moments of quiet, I brought the loader to a stop. I cut the main lights and turned on the lamp I'd brought. I then lowered the bucket to the ground so I could check on Aadesh. He was quickly out and around the cab before I had a chance to exit.

"Are you sure id is being safe do stop here?"

He must've seen the blood on my face, because he ran to the bucket and retrieved some bandages we had requisitioned from the first-aid room. I applied a medium-sized one to my chin. I'd live, but I was going to have a nice scar once it healed. Assuming I lived long enough.

After applying the bandage, I ventured a look at Aadesh standing just below the cab. He shook so hard I thought he might crack the ice. "Are you alright, bro?" I asked.

"Yes. I believe I killed at least do people."

"You saved us."

"I sdopped using the scope." He pulled his hood away from his head.

I smiled. "Good call." He had a perfect, bloody ring the exact diameter of the scope around his left eye.

"Upon my firsd shod, de bidch nearly knocked me oud cold. I believed I was going do fall out of de bucked."

"I saw you fall. I hoped for the best, though." I patted him on the shoulder. "Wait until I tell Sam what you did. He's going to shit his pants."

"I am nod sure I feel comfordable dalking aboud killing humans, bud Sam will wery much be shidding."

"Until we can reach the authorities, we have to do what we have to do... ya know?"

"Yes, dad seems do be de case."

I heard groaning coming from just behind the front wheels. The less smart of the two Sniffers, the one who had climbed on the right fender, had gotten caught in the tight space between the front half and the back half of where the loader pivots in the middle. His left arm was gone, and it looked like he'd been sucked into the space just below the axle that connects the transmission and the front transfer case. He was in agony. Aadesh walked close to him, put the barrel of his rifle close to his head, and pulled the trigger. The Sniffer was out of his agony.

I looked at Aadesh. He looked at me. "Id's eider us or dem. I choose us, bro," he said.

Not sure what to say, I said, "Let's go find our friends."

Aadesh nodded.

Chapter 8

While I was growing up, there was no time for make-believe. There was reality, and then there was Mom's version of hard reality. There was nothing in between at my house. "Wait until you grow up, you little sonofabitch. You're going to be on welfare and have a bunch of snot-nosed kids running around."

That was mom's go-to saying when she thought I was questioning her lack of success in life. How dare I wonder why we didn't have food on Friday? Was it such a bad thing, wondering why I had two shirts and one pair of jeans to last most of the school year? Little Jimmy had a sleeping bag and curtains in his room, not to mention fucking Legos. Actually, more Legos than a kid could put together in a lifetime. "I guess his mom is better than me, ain't she? You can't go back over there. They're putting crazy shit in your head."

God forbid I wanted Legos. I can remember my friend brought his laser tag setup to my house one day. "Mom, see what Bobby has. Can I have one?"

"You're too damn old for stupid toys, you little bastard. You can't be a kid all your life." Hell, I would've been happy being a kid until I was nine, but I guess that was too much to ask.

When I started hanging out with Avery in the sixth grade, he offered a refuge; or, well, his parents did. We were an odd couple. His parents were well off, and my parents weren't. Most parents who lived in a neighborhood like theirs would've been leery about their son hanging out with someone from the trailer park. Maybe what made the difference was that our trailer park was called Palm Villa. That sounds like a nice place, right? It wasn't. They never judged me for living there. They treated me, to my mom's dismay, just like one of their own.

I was introduced to Star Wars, Star Trek, and all kinds of shows with the word Star in them. I wasn't entirely receptive to begin with. "What the fuck is the hairy dude, and how the hell do they understand what he's saying?" I'd ask. Besides having a dirty mouth, I didn't have much imagination about things, that was for sure, but I loved it there. I even came to appreciate science fiction, even if I didn't always understand it or relate to it in any apparent way.

Looking back at it now, there was this odd duality that existed at the time: Mom's notion of reality, what life was going to be no matter how hard you tried or strived; and the world of make-believe, the world that mom couldn't imagine for herself, much less for her children. Even with Avery's disability, his parents never told him what he couldn't do. They focused instead on what he could do, which, in their eyes, was anything he wanted, even following the trailer park kid around the world drilling for oil.

Some of that optimism transferred over to me. I suppose that's some of why I left Indiana to begin with. I wanted to find a world I could create. Not the world that was predetermined for me. Sure, I struggled with old ghosts, bouts of being a terrible person, and, sometimes, just plain sucking at life; but, I finally found who I wanted to become once I settled into a normal life in East Texas.

Having Avery there only sweetened the pot. He was my best friend, and I loved him more than I did my own brother. The circumstances that led him to Texas weren't good ones. Under different conditions, Avery and I would've parted ways after high school. He would've become a hugely successful tech guy, and I would've stayed the average guy I had always been. But life has a way of throwing a monkey wrench into the lives of good people – even good people who happened to be as wealthy as Avery's parents. It had to do with his sister and dad, but that's a story I'll save for another time.

So, life in Texas had been going well. Hell, I'd almost go as far as saying I'd finally had life figured out. I was even beginning to understand the demons that haunted me. But there I was in Barrow, feeling like I was back at Avery's watching Star Wars again for the first time; like I was grappling with two different worlds all over again. Except this time, the world did seem to be intractable and preordained, just like mom had always said it would be, but with a huge fucking twist.

Avery rubbed his bitten hand, oblivious to everything around him except the dead body lying on the floor, and the dire uncertainties inextricably linked to it. The body was exacting a psychological toll on him, and it needed to be moved as quickly as possible.

I placed my hand on his shoulder. He flinched, looked up at me, and diverted his attention back to the body. "You're going to be okay, bud. I promise."

Never taking his eyes off the Gray, he nodded absently.

"Titouan." I flicked my chin towards the guy on the floor, insinuating that I needed help moving his body.

He thought about it for a second before walking over to the body. We drug it over to the corner of the building, as far away from Avery as the square footage allowed. I grabbed one of the other tarps still lying on the floor and began covering the body with it.

"Should we?"

"Should we what?"

"Should we, you know... stab him in the head?"

Fifteen hours ago, I would've laughed. Fifteen hours later and anything seemed possible. "I don't know." I rubbed my cold, glove-less hands together, trying to create enough heat to feel my fingers—to feel good about something. "Tish should have a knife in her bag. See if she'll let you use it."

By the look on his face, I think he thought I was going to do it. He'd brought it up. If he wanted to de-zombie it, I wouldn't stop him, but I didn't want any part of it. He nodded that he'd take care of it. I nodded in return and walked over to where Tish worked on Sam.

From my vantage point, it was hard to see just how severe his injury was, but considering it needed several stitches, it was safe to say it was bad enough. The Gray had to be strong as hell to puncture through three layers of clothing and still do that much damage. I would've asked Tish how bad it was, but it didn't seem like good bedside manner.

In between stitches, Tish wiped her eyes with her coat sleeve. She was a mess. We were all stressed and scared, but Tish seemed to be most affected. "You got a second, Tish?"

She nodded and said, "Almost finished." She wrapped the last bit of bandage around Sam's leg, wiped her face with the back of her hand, and walked over to where I waited.

"You okay?" I asked.

She gave me an odd look. "You expect me to be?"

"I just wanted to say sorry about Tom. If I could've done something, I—"

"Can we just drop it?"
"Yeah," I said, a little hurt by the exchange.

She walked away.

Sam gave me a questioning look as I walked towards him. Ignoring the look, I asked him how he was.

"Son, 'at gray fucker done some damage, but I thank I might be able ta walk with a stiff-ass leg. If we have-ta run, 'ough, I'm screwed."

"I've seen worse. Suck it up," I said.

"I can still outrun you, Bubba."

"Seriously, are you okay?"

He knew I wasn't talking just about his leg. "Them Grays... none of 'is seems real. Almost too much, you know?" He shook his head closed his eyes.

I put my hand on his shoulder. "Yeah, I know. We're tough sonofvabitches, though."

For an instant, I saw the old Sam. He opened his eyes, half smiled, and said, "Cept 'em two," flicking his chin towards Avery and Titouan.

I laughed, thinking about the absurdity of what I was getting ready to say. "It took a damn apocalypse for it to happen, but those two seem to have bonded over it."

He shook his head and lay back, trying to relax his leg as best as possible. Finally, he said, "We'll see how long it lasts. Remind Tit about 'em generators and see how close 'ey are."

"You're probably right about that."

As I talked to Sam, I noticed Titouan and Tish having an animated conversation in the far corner of the building. The knife, I thought. Tish launched an angry look my way. Bastard. He was blaming it on me. He must've been persuasive, because she dug a folding knife out of her coat pocket and slammed it into his open palm.

I walked over to Avery. I thought about sitting down next to him, but I wasn't sure I could get up quickly if I needed to. My legs were killing me. Too many years of eating and partying while also sitting behind a desk. I decided I'd make the best out of my pain and stand in between him and Titouan. No need for Avery to see what Titouan was about to do. He was already stressed and worried enough.

Before I had a chance to utter a word, Avery said, "I am freezing."

"Do you feel like getting up and walking around? That'll help."

"No."

"Come on, dude, you're not dying. You have a little bite on your hand," I said, frustrated.

He looked at me as if I was a complete moron. "A bite is how it normally starts. Besides, I would not be dying in a literal sense. It would be more along the lines of a quasi-state between living and dead—somewhere on the life-death continuum."

"Jesus, Avery. Just stop it, okay?"

Avery had a knack for instantly tuning out things he wasn't interested in. I tried to talk to him, but he didn't reply. I used the excuse of buttoning up his coat, so I could get close enough to check his temperature and make sure he was okay. He broke his gaze with whatever held his interest and turned his attention to me. "I am scared." He thumbed towards the not-completely-out-of-sight body. "I could very well turn into one of those."

"I'm not going to let anything happen to you. We'll make it to Miley's, and we'll figure all this shit out."

He scanned my face but didn't offer any kind of Avery-esque reply. Instead, he said, "I need to close my eyes for a few moments."

"No. No, you're not going to do that," I said, remembering what Tom had said before he'd fallen asleep. I looked at everyone, and said, "We leave in fifteen minutes. We can't stay here." I hoped if I could keep him moving, nothing would happen to him. When I banged my head when I was a kid, the doctor told my mom not to let me go to sleep for a while. I thought about that for some reason, as if those two things were even remotely related.

Maybe I was being as irrational as Avery was, but it was my job to make sure he was taken care of and protected. That, and if anyone was ready for something like this, it was Miley. I'd heard rumors that he was a prepper, even though I'd never seen much evidence of it, aside from the numerous guns he collected and that were always on display around his office. Even if it wasn't true, we came to Barrow to see Miley, and that's what we were going to do. If anyone else had a better plan, I was open to listening. Besides, there hadn't been any shots fired for a while, and that was our litmus test for leaving.

"Avery is going to be okay. Why do we have to rush?" Tish asked.

I pulled her aside, and while keeping an eye on Avery, told her what Tom had said before he'd turned—or whatever had happened to him. She told me I was acting crazy.

"William," she said in a lowered voice. "Avery thinks he's turning into a zombie, and you're not dissuading me at all." She laughed while shaking her head. "I'm quite sure, and I can't believe I'm even saying this aloud, zombies don't stab people. Christ, William, they're not even real." She paused for effect. "You're making things worse, all around."

"What do you mean?"

In her moment of frustration, she blurted out mine and Titouan's plan to stab the Gray in the head, back at the maintenance building. Well, mostly Titouan's. "You seriously told Titouan to stab the guy in the head?"

"It wasn't my idea—"

Not letting me finish throwing Titouan under the bus, she yelled, "There are no fucking zombies."

Shit.

Well, the secret was out of the bag. So much for hiding what Titouan did from Avery. "What's done is done. I don't believe he was, you know, a zombie, Tish," I gave Avery a reassuring glance, "but I refuse to take chances right now."

She stifled a laugh. "But you are taking chances... with all our lives, and you're doing it because of h..." She, for whatever reason, even though she'd already inflicted the damage, saw fit to lower her voice as she pulled me a little farther away from Avery. "Because of Avery. Just be honest."

In a total dick move, I said, "Were you thinking about everyone when you duct-taped that woman's mouth shut back at the house?"

She shot me a hard stare. I thought she was going to punch me, but she managed to calm herself after a few deep breaths. "There are moments when you sound like Titouan. What I did back there was for us and our sanity."

"I shouldn't have said that. I'm sorry," I told her, putting my hand on her shoulder. She jerked away like I had a fresh case of Ebola. And I didn't blame her, really.

Gunshots rang out in the distance. These weren't the single shots we'd heard earlier. These were fired in rapid succession, from what sounded like an automatic weapon, and from just down the street.

"'At ain't yer garden-variety feller with a huntin rifle. 'At's gotta be military," Sam said.

"That's good, right?" Titouan asked.

"As long as 'ey our guys, it's great. The way thangs are goin, 'ough, it might be the damn Japs or Jihadi fellers," Sam said.

"It's got to be safer around them than it is in here," Titouan said.

"Assuming we don't get hit by a stray bullet or an antsy trigger-finger as we approach," I said, not feeling as confident as Titouan.

"I say we go, too," Tish said.

"Huh?" I said, not believing what I was hearing, especially considering how adamant she was about not going just a little while earlier.

"Who else would have weapons like that?"

Titouan liked what Tish was saying. He was gathering his things.

"You hear 'at?" Sam panted.

A revving engine could be heard, followed by a loud crash. "Yeah."

After maybe ten seconds the roaring diesel faded, the void filled with yet another round of intense automatic gunfire. After several minutes of that, there were three pops, followed by silence.

"'Miley's, son. Has ta be," Sam said, trying to stand but struggling due to his injury.

"If the military is there, that's where we need to be," Titouan said.

"It's risky. And I don't like it, but—" I stopped mid-sentence. Avery was nodding off again. I ran over to him and tried to shake him awake, but he was soundly asleep, or sure seemed to be. I got within inches of his face and was yelling for him to wake up. Without warning, his eyes jerked open.

"How did the soldiers get here?" He asked.

"What?" I said. My heart felt like it was beating out of my chest. "You scared me, dammit."

Ignoring my panic-induced moment, he repeated, "Where did the soldiers come from, and how did they get here? There are no land routes other than open tundra into Barrow. That diesel engine you heard almost certainly didn't have anything to do with bringing those soldiers here."

Titouan's mind was made up. He didn't care about Avery's very valid point about how the military had gotten here. He was ready to leave, and that was all there was to it.

Go figure. Avery and Titouan's alliance was beginning to weaken.

I had serious doubts about leaving the maintenance building. Sure, as the curious Gray had proved earlier, we were easy fodder inside the confines of the shack. But we were also so banged up, especially Sam and his cut leg, that we were in no shape to be running from the Grays, either. It boiled down to a single point. If more than one or two Grays attacked us, we would die, and it didn't matter if we were inside or outside the building. At least if we were up and moving, Avery would have to remain awake. Whether it was right or wrong, that was why I decided to leave the shack.

***

Even though the moon shined big and bright, darkness assaulted me. I was having a tough time breathing. I knew it was due to a panic attack, but that knowledge couldn't undo the anxiety. Along with the anxiety, another old friend had come to the party: that bastard, depression. With depression creeping its way in, childhood memories soon followed, creating a triad of bullshit that was making a terrible situation even worse.

I've never liked the dark. Much of this could be traced back to my youth, and specifically on a camping trip with my friends. It was supposed to have been a great adventure, being that it was my first real excursion away from home. It was the first night I'd ever spent away from family.

We sat around the fire telling scary stories until deep into the night. When everyone had exhausted their repertoire of tales and was ready to go to sleep, my friends thought it would be funny if they made me sleep outside the tent by myself. They knew I'd never spent the night with any of them, and that I was afraid of the dark, which is exactly why they did it. It was no fun otherwise.

I was so terrified, I didn't sleep a wink. When they awoke the next morning, I was curled up into a ball just outside the tent, crying and having pissed my pants because I was afraid to get up and relieve myself. From then on out, I was Pee Pee Le Pew. I didn't escape that nickname until I left Indiana. That pain I felt so many years ago seemed to resonate that night, opening a well of emotions I'd for so long repressed.

Even before the camping trip, I'd been afraid to sleep alone in my own house. My parents, on many occasions, awoke to find me on their bedroom floor. Not understanding what to do with me, they stopped me from sleeping in their room. They said I was too old to act like a baby. Maybe I was. I was thirteen at the time.

A couple of years later, my grandpa died. I hadn't known him all that well, but what memories I had of him were good ones. So, I was excited to go stay for a few weeks with my grandma during summer vacation. The impetus of the trip was to allow me to get to know my grandma and help her cope with her loss. I was sure another important part was to push me out of the nest for a bit of a test flight on my own. I'm sure my parents didn't want to take care of me the rest of my life. They barely took care of me then.

The first night I was there, I remember being really embarrassed to ask but too afraid not to, for grandma to leave the light on. I'll never forget the look she gave me. It wasn't anger or embarrassment or anything bad. It was one of warmth, but one also tinged with the look of someone who had been reminded of significant loss.

She came over and sat on the side of the bed next to me. "You knowed yer grandpa worked in the coal mines, didn't ya?"

I told her I did.

"He hated 'em, but they wasn't much else fer a man ta do, and he had me and yer momma ta take care of." She stopped for a few moments and gathered her thoughts. "A man's gotta do what a man's gotta do. You hafta understand 'at." She smiled at me. "He went every day goin on thirty years... worked his hands bloody so we had 'nough ta eat and a place ta sleep. He was a good man. I wont you ta never forget 'at."

I nodded.

I thought she was finished. Instead, she straightened her night coat before cinching it a little bit tighter around her. "Yer granddaddy was a easy goin man—a good man—but not strong of mind, ya know. As bad as 'at cramped dark hole in the ground was on 'im, it was the other thangs that was worse. The long dark is what killed him."

She hesitated as if she might be telling my young ears too much. "Life wore on 'im. He didn't always know what ta do with all his feelins – couldn't handle 'em, ya know. He finally took up drinkin hard liquor 'bout the time yer momma was in the third grade. People thank drunks are weak. Hell, I like ta see some of 'em people work in 'em mines long as he did."

She realized she'd gone off-subject. She gave me a toothless smile, and started again. "The drinkin didn't help... Nothin did. The smile vanished as she finished. "William... Son, as bad as thangs can get sometimes, it's awful easy ta get ta doin things ta try to make yerself feel better. 'Ey ain't no outs—ain't no easy fixes. 'Specially drink. Don't go down 'at same road yer granddaddy did. You hafta find yer light and hold on ta it tight. You hafta ta find yer reason ta live."

I was sad because she was sad, but I didn't really grasp what she was saying at the time. Three years later, after I'd suffered my fair number of bouts with depression, and while going through my grandparents' things, and after she'd passed away, my mom told me how grandma had been so worried about me. She'd told my mom, "The long dark is goin ta get 'at boy." Grandma couldn't call depression by its name. There was too much stigma attached to that word with people her age. You were just lazy, weak-minded, or worse. Instead, she called it the long dark.

Mom being mom, of course, gave me her opinion on things. "I got it. You just have to be tougher than it is. But it don't much matter... You aren't going to amount to anything, anyway." Mom should have been a motivational speaker.

It was a hell of a crazy time to be thinking about all of that, but it was relevant. Before, I'd lived up to mom's nonexistent expectations. I'd done all kinds of stupid shit, trying to escape my demons. The only reason I did so well with Miley was because I craved his attention. He was rich and powerful and had pulled himself up from nothing. He represented exactly the opposite of what my mom expected from me, which is mostly why I did anything he asked, good or bad. For my near-endless loyalty, he rewarded me with a wad of cash. In that I made a great deal of money, for me anyway, I'd become successful, but I would've traded that cash for an ounce of direction.

But that night, even as I struggled with the past, anxiety, and the inherent dangers in this new world, a strength I'd never felt began to swell from some uncharted place from within. I knew in that moment that all that mattered was really the same thing that had always mattered: the people I cared about. I was going to do everything in my power to protect my friends. That was my new purpose.

We would fight this darkness together, and we would live.

"William," I heard Sam anxiously whisper. "Snap out of it, son." He pointed to our left, to a house just off Okpik Street. Someone was inside, and whoever it was had a lantern burning in one of the front rooms. The lantern light and the person weren't the problems. The several dark silhouettes milling outside of the house potentially were.

There was a small, dilapidated building adjacent to the house with the light on. We crouched behind it as we decided whether what was happening posed a threat.

"What do you guys think?" I asked.

Sam looked at the airport security fence to our right before saying, "Not much room ta maneuver, and nowhere ta hide if they up ta no good. I don't know, boys. 'Ey'll see us if we try ta walk by."

"The military is just down the street. I say we make a run for it," Titouan said, agitated that we were waiting around.

"No, we're not going to do that," I said.

Titouan shot me a hateful look.

"Besides the fact that those are probably Grays attacking that house, do you really want to take off running towards a bunch of men with guns?"

Titouan looked away and sighed.

Whoever held the lamp carried it to a different room in the house facing us. A dark outline of someone could be seen just outside the newly lit window. As soon as the lamplight illuminated the rear window, the dark silhouette could be seen looking in through the window from the outside.

"Somethin is 'bout ta go down, boys," Sam said.

"We have seen this before. They seem to be coordinating these attacks. It is hard to cover all the entrances, so they attack multiple egresses. Fascinating," Avery said.

"Did you wipe, boy? 'Cause, by the look on yer face back at the buildin and house, you probably pooped twice. Fascinatin, my ass," Sam said.

Avery popped his knuckles and refused to look Sam in the face. "Their behavior is what it is. I can separate my fear from my fascination."

"Dammit," I said, "not now."

"Maybe the military is clearing that house?" Titouan asked.

Straining to see details that were simply not discernible from our distance, I said, "I doubt that very seriously."

Suddenly, the shadowy figure smashed the window. There was a scream and then another, followed by the cries of what I hoped wasn't a baby. There was a spat of gunshots fired out of the window; the flashes lit the room and created supersonic pops as they sped past, too close for comfort. Whoever tried to get into the back room got a nasty surprise, but the safety of those in the house was as tenuous as the front door was capable of holding back the gaggle of bodies punching, pressing, and kicking at it.

"There's yer answer, Tit. Ain't no damn military."

I checked the rifle, making sure it had a round in the chamber. I didn't want the same thing that happened to Sam to happen to me. "Give me any spare ammo you have in that bag, Titouan," I told him.

"What the hell ya doin, son?"

"Didn't you hear the baby crying? I have a gun, and I'm going to help," I said, putting the ammo Titouan gave to me in my pocket.

"What are we supposed to do?" Titouan asked.

"Get your asses to Miley's. Even if those aren't Grays attacking that house, and I'm pretty sure it is, the noise will draw them in soon enough," I said.

"Which is why you shouldn't do 'is, William, ya damn fool," Sam pleaded.

"After what happened to Tom... I can't just leave them to die. I'm going to try to help," I said.

Sam tried one last time to stop me. "Son, don't do 'is. You can't go comparin 'is with what happened ta Tom."

"It feels awfully damn close to me," I said.

Sam spit. "You a bull-headed sonofabitch. Get yer ass ta Miley's soon as ya can. I mean 'at."

"I'll be right behind you guys. Now go before more show up."

I patted Avery on the shoulder and began walking towards the house. Between my girth and lack of anything that might hide my approach, I was perfect fodder for either a bullet or something much more dreadful. I had the gun up and ready. Twenty yards into my mission, I turned and took one more look at my friends. Sam was leading them away, just as I'd asked. Not happy, but doing it all the same.

I turned back towards my quarry. Some things dawned on me in rapid succession. One, I had no fucking clue what I was doing. Two, I was scared out of my wits. Three, I'd just sent my friends off into the unknown, for people who I'd never met and who might be dead by the time I got myself into a position to help. Four, I was majorly having second thoughts.

But then there was this weird channel that opened in my mind. All it was playing was the crying baby. Thanks, conscious—screwing me again. I said, "fuck it," and picked up my pace.

I was a mess, yet coherent and rational enough to angle my approach in such a manner I hoped made the Grays on the porch unable to see me. The smell part I couldn't control, so I tried not to worry about it. I was close to the broken-out window. I didn't want to have my brains blown out, so I kept out of viewing range.

I could clearly see the forms on the porch as I peeked around the corner of the house. Now what? I had five rounds in the magazine and one in the chamber. I counted seven Grays. If I were extremely lucky, I could hit three or four of them before I'd have to reload. I only had the one magazine in the rifle, which meant I'd have to load the rounds individually into the mag. That wouldn't work. I'd still be trying to reload while they were piling on me doing whatever it is they do.

Shit. The front door exploded. Decision time. I didn't have all day to weigh my options. It amounted to run or gun, at that point. I chose the latter.

Footfalls pounded against the flooring inside. It sounded like at least one of them fell as they fought to get into the house, the floor creaking with every step. One of them bellowed in anger. There were curses and screaming followed by more pounding fists. Whoever was in the back room had barricaded themselves in, but for how long was anybody's guess. If the front door was any indication, the answer was not long at all.

"Take the baby and go," I heard a man pleading just inside the room with the broken-out window. A woman told him she wasn't leaving. "You have to go now. Please," he repeated.

The door was splintering and would give way soon. Without thinking and breaking the rule about not wanting my brains blown out, I ran to the window and was about to yell into the house when there was a flash and a deafening blast, or blasts. I was disorientated. My left ear felt like it had exploded. I don't remember how I'd ended up on the ground; I just knew that I was. I checked all my parts to make sure they were still there and working. I'm not sure how the person had missed, but I was damn happy he or she had. I heard cursing in the room where the blast had come from.

I rolled away from the window and got to my feet. From the side of the window frame, I called to the people inside, "Don't shoot, dammit. I'm trying to help." Two more shots. A Gray, or at least I thought it was a Gray, wailed. "Go. I'll hold them back," came a man's voice.

"Please let me help you," I said.

Three rapid shots were fired, followed by desperate words. "I only have a couple bullets left. You have to go!"

It sounded like a dresser or something heavy was being pushed across the floor, along with scraping wood, picture frames, and other knickknacks falling to the floor. "Go."

I heard footsteps from behind me. And sniffing—loud sniffing. I turned only to see a big hulk of a Gray bearing down on me. He was on me before I could react. The next thing I knew, I was on the ground, and he was on top of me, pounding the living hell out of me with his fists. I was disoriented from the heavy blows, but I knew I had to do something fast, or I was dead. I reached for the rifle that had been knocked out of my hands, but couldn't reach.

The dark cloak of unconsciousness began to envelop me like a fog, bringing with it an odd relief.

I heard a muffled pop. The smell of death was in the air, but not mine. The veil that had enveloped me with peace had suddenly been ripped away. In its place came the piercing cries of an infant and heavy snowflakes falling on my battered face.

Using every ounce of strength I had left, I managed to push the limp body off of me. I struggled to my feet. I closed and opened my eyes, trying to get them to focus in the low-light conditions. A woman with a swaddled infant in one arm and a pistol in the other stood a couple feet away from me. A pistol that just happened to be pointed directly at me.

It had begun snowing heavily again.

I had my rifle pointed at the woman but didn't realize it until I followed her eyes towards it. I lowered it. The woman didn't immediately return the favor with her pistol. "Thanks for saving me," I said, nervously, not sure I was saved just yet. Only when there was a loud crash from inside the house did she finally lower her pistol.

The man cursed. The woman paused in indecision. She took a long look back towards the house.

"Don't do it," I told her.

I labored under the two or three steps between us and grabbed hold of her arm and tried to drag her away from the house, but there was something slippery on her jacket, and I nearly fell on my ass as I lost my grip.

"We have to go," I implored.

The baby was screaming. We were going to have every Gray in Barrow on us if she couldn't stop the crying. First thing first, we had to get away from the house. The man was quickly losing the battle, and after they were finished with him, we'd be next.

I grabbed her wrist, which luckily wasn't slimy like her coat, and pulled her away from the window. After a few steps, she arrested her arm from my grip, obviously not trusting me, but she nevertheless moved with purpose, never more than just a few steps behind me.

We hurried towards the dilapidated building where I'd just moments earlier sent my friends off into the unknown. There was no sign of them. I hoped they were okay, but I had bigger problems. I was getting ready to tell the woman if she didn't manage to quiet the child, we were dead. Before I could utter the first word, the baby had stopped. I mean, she just stopped. No whimpering. Nothing.

The man in the house screamed. He was losing the valiant battle he'd been waging, and as soon as the Grays were finished, they'd be looking for their next target. A single pop could be heard from the direction of the house. The screaming stopped. I quickened my pace.

Chapter 9

A group of Grays could be heard somewhere off to our right. We huddled behind a garbage dumpster while they sniffed and snorted their way past us. Two of the Grays near the end of the pack splintered off from the rest and got uncomfortably close to the dumpster. They looked disoriented. One spun in circles before falling to the ground. He didn't get up. I wasn't sure if he was dead, but he wasn't moving. The other wondered aimlessly off in another direction.

After watching the befuddling show, I glanced over at the child. Her poor little face was covered in snow. Jesus, I thought, could you not wipe the poor thing off. A street over, there was a business with a small portico that would provide a much-needed respite from the elements, and hopefully allow the woman some time to come to her senses. It would have the added benefit of allowing me to think.

Once safely there, the woman, at my urging, listlessly dusted the snow off her child. After wiping the child's face, she tried to clean her own, but the smooth fabric of her coat, coupled with the weird coating on her sleeves, didn't function well as a snot rag. Instead of wiping the snot and tears away, her coat sleeve had the effect of smearing them all over her face.

The woman wasn't much of a talker. I asked her on at least two occasions if she'd been injured. She stared blankly in any direction but mine, not bothering to acknowledge my words. I hoped it was just shock and that she would come around. I focused instead on things that aimed to do harm to us while she re-swaddled her baby in a pair of thick, pink blankets. After waiting for her to finish with the child, I asked her if she was ready to continue. She looked irked for being asked. She did, however, give me a slight nod.

I'd walked several feet before noticing she wasn't following me. Instead, she stood under the portico, fidgeting with something in her pocket. I couldn't see what the hell she was doing, but it wasn't nearly as important as getting her ass going. I quickly walked to where she stood and reiterated how she needed to follow me. She gathered up what resolve she could muster and finally did as I asked.

The woman cleared her throat. I looked at her, expecting her to say something, but she didn't. We walked a bit farther before she finally spoke. "Where are we going?"

I knew she had a child, but she was really dragging ass. Not only that, but on the rare occasion she did talk to me, she spoke too loudly because she wouldn't, for whatever reason, walk near me. I stopped. Once she finally got close enough, I said, "The pancake."

"What's the pancake?"

That was weird, I thought. The joke of Barrow had been Miley's building. One of the local tour companies had even added the monstrosity as a stop. When we were on leave in town, and one of the locals heard we worked for Miley, laughs and jeers almost always followed. I assumed everyone knew about the pancake. "You not from around here?" I asked.

She paused for a moment, and I wondered if she was going to stonewall me some more. Instead, she finally said, "My husband and I just moved back from Dillingham to help out with his sick parents. Why?" She replied, barely audible this time and near emotionless.

"Just curious."

Miley's office building was called the pancake because it looked like three huge, double-wide trailers had their roofs lopped off and were then stacked on top of one another. Throw in an industrial-strength double-door on the bottom floor, a few narrow, shuttered windows, some underpinning that matched the shutters to try to hide the metal stilts that elevated it above the permafrost, this God-awful orange paint to round out the decor, and that was Miley's office building.

She gave me a quick glance before looking away.

"We're going to Miley Corp. It's not too far from here."

"I think I know the place, now that you mention it," She paused. "I'm... I'm glad we're going there. It seems like a safe place," she said, trying to contort her face into something bordering on a smile.

Something struck me as off about her, but I couldn't put my finger on what that something was. "Yeah."

We crouched against a fence extending a good portion of the northern perimeter of the runway, presumably erected to keep fools and drunks from getting hit by planes on landings and takeoffs. H Street was just a few feet away from us on our left, and Miley's office was not much more than a block or two away to the east, on the other side of D Street.

If we had gotten there before the snow had begun falling again, I would've been able to see Miley's office building from where we stood, but with the fresh round of thick snow, I could barely see twenty feet in front of me. "We're going to have to move. I can't see anything from here."

"I won't be able to keep her from crying," she said sharply.

I nodded. "I should probably know your name. If I've got to call for you or something, it's just going to be a little weird, saying, hey, you," I said, kind of sort of trying to cut the tension.

She acted like she didn't want to tell me it, but after an awkward few seconds, she finally said it was Kelley.

"Well, Kelley, my name is William. If the baby cries, we'll figure something out, okay?"

She was a woman of few words. She didn't bother replying to me. Instead, she indicated she'd heard me by slightly nodding her head, not bothering to even make eye contact. She was sort of an angry Avery, I thought.

Over the howl of the wind, I was sure I heard voices just up the street from us. "Did you hear that?"

She shook her head. "No."

I hoped it was my friends. I listened a few more moments but heard nothing.

I'd like to say I was a great leader during those early days. I could imagine my dopey self on a poster. I'd be holding a pistol or maybe a big-ass sword. There'd be a woman holding onto my leg; hell, maybe it would be Kelley—lord knows she was pretty enough to be on a poster. I'd point that sword in the direction of my enemies, and my army of lesser men would charge into the void and vanquish them. That would be kick-ass. It would also be the biggest lie ever told.

The reality of the situation? My leadership was less optimal than that. Sam would've called it "hog shit in a nun's bellybutton", or described my ineptitude in some other nonsensical way. The fact was, I didn't known what to do.

We were within running distance of Miley's. Looking down at the poor baby, I remember thinking how she might not make it if we didn't hurry. But if we hurried and ran into a mess of Grays, they would kill her even more quickly than the bite of the bitter cold.

***

There was a blue duplex just across the street from Miley's office building. It had stairs leading to a small landing and entrance to the upstairs apartment. The landing would provide an excellent vantage point over the surrounding area. A few minutes up there, scoping the area seemed like a better option than just running for our lives and hoping Miley's was safe.

Under the steps leading to the second-floor apartment was a small, mostly-enclosed cubbyhole just big enough for Kelley and baby. It had wide strips of latticework covering the railing and would give adequate cover from the wind and snow. I let her know I was going to climb to the top to get a better look. She absently nodded. I was starting to grow on her.

The surprise of hearing what I thought was a buzzing cell phone stopped me in my tracks. More specifically, I heard the reverberations of a vibrating cell phone off the wooden lattice of the porch. "Did you hear that buzzing?" I asked, walking around to where she sat.

"I don't know what you're talking about... I didn't hear anything," she said.

Either I was going crazy, or Kelley was deaf. She hadn't heard the voices I know I heard, and she hadn't heard the loud, vibrating sound coming from two feet away from her. I was exhausted mentally and physically, my nerves were shot, but, by god, my ears still worked. I decided to let it go. There were more important matters to attend to.

The landing was a complete dud. The advantage of height was overridden mightily by darkness and snowfall. The only thing it did was give me time to feel terrible for all the crappy decisions I'd made up until that point. I had endangered my friends' lives. Not only that, but I'd picked up two other people I couldn't take care of.

A lot of what I was feeling was fear of the unknown and the hopelessness that was born out of it. At that exact moment, hope only seemed to exist inside the confines of Miley's ugly-ass building. There was no plan past that. Therefore, no hope existed beyond its orange exterior.

You know how you feel when you buy a Powerball ticket? Statistically, you know you aren't going to win, but that doesn't stop you from thinking you could be holding a winning ticket. I wanted to savor my numbers a little while longer. I didn't want to find out I'd lost, because everyone is a potential winner until they're not. But it was time. I was going to have to suck it up and find out. It was time to play the numbers I had.

I quickly made my way down to where Kelley sat. Where was the baby, I wondered? Before I could say anything, Kelley said, "I needed to feed her. She was getting fussy."

Sure enough, she had her inside her parka. "Oh, okay—I'm, uh, I'm going back up there until you're finished."

"It'll just be a few more minutes."

"Sure." More time to savor my numbers.

She seemed to be trying to be nice to me. For a moment, I felt guilty for the way I felt about her. I'd hired a lot of people in my day, though, and my record was pretty good, especially given I didn't always have top-tier people to choose from. I was confident in my gut, and it was screaming not to trust her, especially since I was sure she'd lied to me about the cell phone. Having said all of that, I was willing to delay my conclusions about her until a later time, especially considering she had just horribly lost her husband.

But still, if all the electronics were down, how in the hell did she have a working cell phone?

As soon I got back to the landing, I heard a crash to my left, followed by the sounds of multiple windows being broken out. Soon after, I heard the crunch of footsteps in the snow directly below the landing. My first thought was of Kelley running off with the baby. I looked to where the noise seemed to be coming from, and it wasn't Kelley. There was a brief respite of sound, and then I was inundated with the crunching of hundreds of footsteps in the snow.

"The fuck," I said under my breath. A completely naked Gray walked by, no more than ten feet away from the duplex. I quickly switched off my headlamp, so he wouldn't see me. He was closely followed by Grays in various forms of dress. The naked man was in the minority, but others were almost as scantily clad as he was. If they were affected by the cold, they didn't act like it.

Grays filed out between the houses all along D Street before congregating in the street next to Miley's office. Without the extra light from my headlamp, I couldn't see far enough to get an exact number. Considering the number of footsteps and the amount of sniffing and snorting I heard, there had to be a lot of them.

Why hadn't I fucking gone when I'd had the chance?

"William," Kelley whispered from below me. I quickly scanned below us to see if any Grays had been alerted by her voice, but the ones I could see seemed unaffected. I quickly but quietly made my way down the steps, crouching to stay below the railing on the way to where she sat safely in her little nook with the baby still inside her parka.

"I can't see anything from here. What's going on?" She asked, being a hell of a lot cooler than I was.

I got as close to her as was comfortable before whispering, "Grays. We're blocked from Miley's, at least from here, anyway."

She gave me a questioning look. "Grays?"

"The monsters," I huffed, leaving it at that.

She nodded.

A Gray sniffed dangerously close. He must have heard me. I put my hands out in front of me, palms towards her, letting her know to stay put. I duck walked to the steps leading down off the porch. My legs burned at almost any new activity. So much so, that my right leg finally locked up, causing me to have to stop and stretch it for a moment before continuing. I crawled on my hands and knees the rest of the way to the steps.

I peeked around the railing to my right, then chided myself for letting out a quick gasp. No more than five feet away, stood at least four Gray stragglers. They were curious about something; they sniffed the air relentlessly, but for whatever reason, they seemed content to sniff in place. That they were agitated, let me know they knew something was up, but they were having a tough time figuring out exactly what it was they were curious about. One of them yelped like a dog. That was new.

There was a noise somewhere to the south of the duplex. Who in the hell would be stupid enough to make that much noise? I wondered. It sounded like a metal pipe being smacked against the airport safety fence. There was a buzz of grunts and inhuman sounds beginning near the fence and cascading all up and down the line of Grays in the street. This was followed by many sprinting towards the sound. Much to my dismay, there were still plenty of grunts and snorts from Grays who hadn't left. Still, I couldn't help wondering if the noise hadn't thinned the ranks in front of us enough that we might be able to sneak through the line.

My manhood already gone due to my inability to walk upright, I crawled back to the nook. I let Kelley know I was going to see if there was a way forward to Miley's and that, if there wasn't, I was going to try to clear a way back to safety. "Get your pistol ready, just in case." She nodded.

I crept down the steps, trying to stay low and quiet enough to go unnoticed. The four steps off the porch were just about the cherry on top for my increasingly uncooperative legs. A lone Gray was off to my right, his back facing me. He was the only one I saw, but there were others. I was sure of that. The Gray in front of me suddenly jerked his head around to the side, sniffing loudly but not moving.

I inched towards D Street. I cursed silently. The Grays in the street were packed in so tightly, there was no way we could make our way through their ranks. I moved a short way towards the airport, but the line was just as thick there. There could've been a thousand or more of them blocking our way. Why had I been so damn stupid and indecisive?

I eased my way back several feet from the street. As bad as I hated to think about it, the maintenance building was the safest bet. We might be able to break into a closer house, but who knew what we might find inside. I decided on the maintenance building. It was the safest bet.

I would need to clear a path back to the maintenance building. I wasn't sure how I would do it, though. I couldn't exactly ask them nicely to disperse in an orderly fashion. I quickly glanced around for bottles, cans, or anything like that I could use to get their attention. Then it dawned on me that even if I were to be able to find things to throw, they weren't going to make enough noise when they hit the snow. That wasn't going to work. I would have to be the noisemaker.

I surveyed a path back to the maintenance building. There were stragglers everywhere. I crept between two of them, miraculously going unnoticed. I moved about twenty more feet before I lightly clapped my hands together. The one closest to me began making odd guttural breaths but didn't initially move. I clapped again, this time a little harder. The last thing I wanted to do was alert the main group in the street.

The Gray jerked his head up and towards my direction, grunted, then sniffed hard and took several unsure steps in my direction. The one next to him grunted and moved, and that prompted the next Gray, and so on and so forth, until I'd managed to move a decent-sized group of them away from the duplex. They were surprisingly easy to move. Too easy.

As per usual, when someone gets overconfident, mistakes are made. I wanted to hurry up and get them out of the way, so I moved farther away from them while clapping my hands harder. I had no reason to worry because the ones following me seemed to lack the ability to find me in the heavy snowfall. Like the one back at the house, not all of them were docile idiots. There were smarter ones out there. I forgot that fact.

I'd moved them far enough away for my escape plan to work, but I decided to clap one more time for good measure. Not long after that last clap, I heard fast footfalls in my direction. Assuming I was the target, I wasted no time trying to get the hell away, but I lost my footing in the snow and fell. My head hit something hard, maybe the rifle, in the snow after my feet slipped out from under me, and I felt like I might black out, again.

The warm, rancid breath I felt on my face and inhaled through my nostrils jolted me back to my senses. The Gray crouched between my spread legs, much closer to the goods than was remotely comfortable. His gray face was covered in dried blood, which reminded me of the lunch lady back at the house. I threw up, most of which ran out of my mouth, down my face, and into my ear. The Gray sniffed and snorted wildly.

Besides his face being the normal gray, it also drooped badly on one side, maybe from a stroke or whatever was causing them to go crazy. His face also seemed to be locked in an almost sorrowful expression, which in no way resembled his demeanor towards me. He grabbed air with his hands, just above me; once, twice, and then repeatedly. I used my elbows to crawl backward a few feet, but he sensed my movement and followed. I could see the silhouettes of at least two of the ones I'd lured away from the duplex, but for whatever reason, they didn't join the fray. I moved again, with the same result. I tried to get up, but he was too close.

If I scooted backward, he moved forward. If I tried to get up, his probing hands would feel me. I'd have to wait for the right moment. Luckily, that moment didn't take long to arrive. The baby began to cry, loudly.

The Gray jerked his head around towards the sound of the screaming infant. I took advantage of my opening. I quickly scooted far enough back that I could maneuver my rifle around for a shot. I aimed at his head, and just as he began to turn his gaze back towards me, I fired. His head exploded above me in a mist of crimson. He lay crumpled between my legs, blood flowing from the massive wound, causing the white snow to turn red.

I was on my knees and trying to regain my footing. "Fuck!" I slipped and fell. I yelled aloud, adrenaline coursing through my body. I reached for the rifle on the ground and used it as a crutch. I was dizzy, but at least upright. I hurried towards the crying baby.

I heard two quick shots, followed by two thuds. Two dead Grays lay crumpled on the ground, still twitching. Kelley was nowhere in sight. I followed the screaming baby, as did every damn Gray in the vicinity. I bowled over a Gray from behind. I homed in on the wailing baby. Kelley was just in front of me. I yelled for her to follow me.

"Miley's," I said quickly, struggling for breaths. At that point, it didn't matter how much noise we made, because the baby had already done, and was still doing, the damage.

There were pounding footsteps a few yards behind me. I turned and fired, clipping the lead Gray in the leg. He cried out in pain as he tumbled in the snow, after losing the use of his nicked leg. Lucky shot to the kneecap, I thought. I slung the rifle over my shoulder and ran as fast as I could for the next thirty or so yards.

I skidded to a stop within a few feet of what used to be the entrance to Miley's office. No! The entire door frame had been pulled out of the structure, leaving a double-door sized opening in the building. The frame lay on the ground, the top-center part bent outward in a sharp V-shape, a chain still attached.

"Fuck," I yelled. There was no one there. Miley's had been broken into. With the doors gone, it wouldn't be safe inside. All of this had been for nothing—there was no place to go now. And my friends... "Fuck!" I repeated. Between the wailing baby and my bellowing curse words, we might've well been circus barkers with bullhorns. Come one, come all; come pummel your baby and washed-up former drill superintendent.

"Where's your boss?" Kelley asked, her voice shaded with worry. Maybe she wasn't a robot, after all.

"I don't know." The Grays were quickly surrounding us. "We're going to have to figure something out quickly."

The lead element was twenty yards and closing. We might've been able to kill a few of them, but that would pull in some of the dumber ones who were struggling to find us. Still, we were going to have to do something. "How many bullets do you have?" I asked. No response. "Get ready to run... and shoot if necessary, but not until then," I said.

"William!" I heard the sweetest voice in the world. It was Tish. "Get in here, now!"

The baby screamed. Kelley fired two quick shots. The Grays fell to the ground, one of which slid to within a foot of me. Kelley was turned and moving towards Tish when I took out the next closest two. Of course, I needed four shots to do it. The pounding feet were close, but it was now or never. I had to run. Just as I was about to be overtaken, I saw a figure walk outside the entrance. There was a pause, then a deafening barrage of shots fired towards the Grays behind me. I was going to make it.

Titouan stepped back inside, slung the rifle over his shoulder, and grabbed the lamp off the ground. Holy shit, Titouan had saved me.

Titouan and Tish led the way forward. Several bodies lay dead on the floor. "Watch the bodies," Titouan said. "And fucking hurry!"

I heard Kelley say something as she stepped over one of them, but I didn't think anything of it. There were five or six of them that I could see. It was hard to see in the relative darkness, but they didn't appear to be Grays.

Once at the top of the stairs, with Grays in the building and on our heels, Tish pulled a thick metal door across the entrance, closing off the stairwell to the second floor. The sound of several Grays slamming against it brought me boundless joy. Fuckers.

Kelley stood like a statue. She held the child loosely in her left arm, while white-knuckling the pistol in her right hand. She was oblivious to everything, including her crying child.

"Are you okay, Kelley?" I asked.

"Let's take this to the third floor. There's heat up there," Tish said, before Kelley had a chance to respond or ignore.

I stood on wobbly legs. I was hurting all over, so badly that I barely made it up the single flight of stairs to the third floor. Warmth. There was heat... and electricity. I heard Tish close another metal door behind me. The clang of it locking was one of the greatest sounds I'd heard in a long time.

The first thing I noticed on the third floor was that all the windows were covered with a dark covering, giving the appearance of complete darkness to anyone trying to look in from the outside. Did I mention that there was heat and electricity? I was confused by that, but I was happy about it.

Avery came out of one of the conference rooms. If memory serves me correctly, it was the same one Miley had demoted me in. He hadn't even bothered taking me into his office. Ah, nice memories to go with my current state of terror and astonishment.

Avery looked me up and down, no expression on his face, not even a blink of an eye, before saying, "Miley wants to see you after you get cleaned up. He will not talk to any of us about what is going on. Only you. And, I might add, you look terrible."

"Good to see you, too, bud... But why won't he talk...?" I realized I saw everyone but Sam. "Where the hell is Sam?" I asked, afraid I'd get an answer I didn't want to hear.

"He's in the conference room, resting," Tish said.

I exhaled. "I was afraid for a second."

"He's fine. Right now, you just need to clean up, and then find out what Miley knows," Tish said.

"He hasn't said a word to you guys?"

A flash of anger flitted across her face. "He's acting weird. He knows something."

"Okay," I said, leaving it at that.

I walked over and peeked into the door in the conference room. Sam seemed to be napping. People sometimes tell you things they think you need to hear. I just wanted to make sure what Tish said wasn't an example of that.

***

I unslung my backpack and took my parka off and placed it on the restroom floor, along with my bloody boots and gloves. It only took a glance in the mirror to see what a mess I was. I couldn't tell if my tri-colored face—purple, red, and black—was from one gigantic bruise or a bunch of smaller ones. I had the gash I'd received from the corner of the table back at the patch, and, to top things off, my left eye was nearly swollen shut. I could also see that the screwdriver wound had stopped bleeding, but damn, it was sore. I looked like shit.

I stayed in the bathroom for what seemed like forever, basking in the wonder that was warm water. I soaked a rag in hot water, draped it over my face, and left it there until it cooled off, and repeated the process several times as I rested on the toilet. It's amazing how much the little things mean after not having them for a brief period.

I was met outside the bathroom door by Titouan and Avery. I dropped my gear by the wall, and before I could ask why the long faces, Titouan said, "That woman you picked up. She was covered in the same mucus the lady back in the house was."

We had both fought with the Grays. It made sense that both of us would be covered with the stuff. "Yeah, my coat is covered with it. So what?"

Avery gave me a skeptical look. "Perhaps."

"Guys, I don't have time for this..." The hallway was empty. "Where are Kelley and Tish?"

Titouan pointed to one of the small supply rooms. "Locked in there," he said.

"If you two have something on your mind, why don't you just cut to it. I'm too damn sore and exhausted to be playing games with you two."

"Sam asked me to check on Tish, but the door was locked. Sounded like they were arguing in there, but they hushed up when I called to them, acting like nothing was wrong," Titouan said.

"Well, maybe nothing was wrong. I have to talk to Miley. I don't have time for this," I said.

Titouan flashed me a look that I recognized from the old Titouan. "Tell him, I said hello."

"I'd rather not talk to him at all, or at least not all cloak-and-dagger like he apparently wants. I'll gladly trade you places."

Titouan shook his head and walked away. That was the Titouan I knew and loved.

I heard a door open down the hall. Tish exited the room and walked over to where Avery and I stood. "Remember, Miley wanted to talk to you."

I nodded, and then said, "Everything okay with Kelley and baby?"

"Yeah, I was just checking them over." She gave Avery a quick glance before settling her gaze on me. "Why do you ask?"

"Just wondering, that's all. The baby was in the cold a long time."

"She'll be okay."

I was relieved to hear that. "Good."

"How is Miley?"

Tish smirked. "Drunk."

***

Miley sat at his desk, looking much more haggard than I'd ever seen him. "Mr. Miley," I said and nodded hello. Miley always preferred to be called Mr. Miley. I'm fairly sure his friends, if he had any, were kept at the same arms-length decorum. He waved me over to have a seat across from him at his oversized desk.

"Hello, William."

There was a long and awkward pause. He took several long drafts from a bottle I recognized. A bottle I couldn't believe he was drinking from. He must've noticed me looking at it.

"When the world goes to shit, you can drink the good stuff. You want a swig?"

"I stopped drinking a while back."

"Prohibition is so cliché, William. Drink with me."

"What's going on here, Mr. Miley?"

He pounded the gaudy decanter on the desk. "I'm getting drunker. That's what's going on."

"In Barrow."

"Do you know this was my brother's favorite? He was much more sophisticated and refined than I'll ever be. Take this bottle of Remy Martin Louis XIII Cognac. Seven thousand dollars I'm holding right here. Even the long name is pretentious as hell. Makes no sense, really, but it makes me think of him. You remember him, right?"

"Yes... I liked your brother a great deal. It was a tragedy what happened to him."

"Too great of a loss to bear, I'm afraid."

"I'm sorry about your brother, but we have other pressing matters, like what the hell is going on."

"I don't know what's happening..." He took another drink. "Well, I might know some of what's happening. I just don't know exactly how."

"What does that mean?"

"I guess it doesn't really matter if I tell you or not. What are you going to do, call the FBI or CIA?" He laughed and took yet another drink.

"I don't understand."

"Did you happen to see the front door of my office?"

"Hard to miss. It's gone."

"Exactly. I was attacked."

"The Grays did that?"

"Grays?" he asked, beginning to laugh.

"Yeah, that's what we're calling them, I guess."

"I prefer monsters."

"Please, Mr. Miley, can you tell me what you know."

He took a giant mouthful of the cognac. So much it trickled from the corner of his mouth onto his shirt and desk. He wiped his face and then pointed to a weapon that I hadn't noticed in the dimly lit room. I wasn't an expert on such things, but I believed it was an AR-15. I remember the magazine more than the actual rifle. It was one of the high-capacity jobs that were popular with the wingnuts who shot up public places. Anyway, it was one of the drum-type magazines—maybe a hundred rounds. "No, the damn Grays, as you call them, didn't pull the door out of the frame. The people who did it were fully-thinking, non-monster sons of a bitches. I took care of them. Except one of them, anyway."

"What the hell are you talking about?"

"I fucked up, William. I got caught up in the wrong things..."

I knew he was drunk, but he was making no sense whatsoever. "I'm exhausted, Mr. Miley."

His eyes narrowed. "I'm trying to explain to you what the fuck is going on. So how about listening to me."

I nodded.

"Everything was going my way. I had a friendly administration—one I helped get elected, I might add," he said, his head tilting heavily to one side as he spoke. "I just needed money. Capital, you know. I mean, the bastards were going to open huge swaths of the Arctic, and I can't take advantage of it. I'm tapped out. I have no liquidity, at all. That's why I sold East Texas. I needed fucking money!"

I was getting ready to say something when he put his hand up, letting me know to be quiet. He then stood up, turned the bottle up, and nearly fell backward in the process. He walked over to the rifle and slung it over his shoulder. Deciding that standing wasn't a good idea, he fell back down in his chair and swigged another long drink before continuing.

"That's why I closed down and sold almost everything that was onshore. The Arctic was the way to the future. I was ahead of all the big boys. I just needed the money. I have contacts in Russia and places worse than Russia. Lots of them. I called in a favor or two, and I was pointed to a group of investors who could help. They offered a deal I couldn't turn down."

All I could muster was, "And the deal was?"

He began to laugh. "All I had to do was hold five containers at the Patch for a few weeks. I'd get loans at rates men like me dream of, and money—more money than you could ever dream of, funneled in through back channels to discrete accounts on a certain small, Pacific island. It was perfect. I was going to ram a gigantic cock right up BP, Exxon, and any other fucker who got in my way. I was going to be on top for once."

I knew exactly what containers he was talking about. "So, the people who guarded those containers weren't government contractors? I guess you just figured us for morons, then?"

"I suppose, since we're honest here, that you're right. We all have to eat a little shit sometimes. I lied to you, and you knew better enough to question things."

"Jesus, Miley."

"I don't remember you ever calling me just Miley."

"All kinds of firsts, I guess."

"To be fair, I didn't know what was in the containers, either. Just like you, I knew better to ask."

"Bullshit. There's a big damn difference between us."

"I suppose you're right. The result is the same, though. We both got fucked."

"So, who attacked you?"

"The people I made the deal with, I'm assuming. Tie up all loose ends. If things were as successful elsewhere as they were here, I'm not sure why it mattered. I guess that's just how they play."

I stood up. It dawned on me that things were much worse than I'd ever imagined. I couldn't believe what I was hearing. My mind raced. Thoughts spun around like they were in a centrifuge, only none separated into anything remotely discernible.

"What the hell do we do?"

"I don't know what you're doing, but I'm leaving Barrow as soon as possible. I already have my things packed and ready to go. I knew you would show up, assuming nothing happened to you, and I wanted to do as best by you as I could... as best as I could before I left. There are supplies in the small conference room. I don't have many weapons, but I gave you what I could spare. Whether you believe it or not..." He paused for a long moment. I thought maybe he was preparing another lie for consumption. "I'm sorry for what I've done."

It was my turn to laugh. "Does it really matter?"

"Probably not..." His hard features softened. With sadness in his voice I hadn't heard since his brother died, he continued. "My girls are in Anchorage. I don't know if they're alive or not. I sent them messages, but they never replied."

"I hope they're okay."

Ignoring what I'd just said, he handed me a piece of paper. "I want to do this for you. Memorize it, because I'm going to burn it before I leave. You were always my favorite, William. I saw you, whether you believe it or not, as almost a son that I never had. I fucked up... and I know this won't fix things, but it's all I can do."

Chapter 10

Everything on Miley's desk that meant something to him was thrown into a duffle bag. The only exception was the empty bottle of cognac—he planned to take extra loving care of that; right down his gullet. He pulled a drawer open and retrieved two handguns. He placed one of them in a holster on his side and gave me the other. "There's ammunition for that in the supplies I'm leaving you." He then told me to follow him, except he didn't lead me through the door that led back into the interior. "Grab a blanket off the couch there and cover-up. It's cold where we're going."

Like in something out of a spy novel, he opened the doors to a large cabinet at the back of the room. Instead of having any kind of office supplies, it opened to a hidden room barely big enough for a normal man to fit through, much less me.

After I squeezed through the door, he closed everything up. I followed him through another door that led to a spiral staircase. It wound the entirety of the three stories. Just off the stairs was another small, rectangular walkway that led to another door. He opened that door and lights automatically flickered on. We were in his personal garage. There was a van, a truck, and two large tracked vehicles inside. One of the tracked vehicles was running and ready to go. I wondered why we weren't asphyxiating, but then, I noticed there were silent exhaust fans on the roof. He'd thought of everything.

He looked at me and smiled. "You can't be in the business that I'm in, make the kinds of deals I've made—not to mention enemies—and not be a lot paranoid."

"Yeah," I said, not knowing what else to say.

He walked over to a large cabinet and retrieved a small backpack. "You'll need this. There's a working radio along with a few other things in there. There's also a phone. Not that it'll do you any good without service, but it's in there."

"How?"

"I already told you, paranoia. Some people say preppers are crazy and that they don't realize it. I suppose I'm the anomaly. I'm crazy, and I know it, but I'm crazy like a fox. I was prepared for this long before I helped cause it."

Crazy like a fox, maybe, but he was definitely drunk as a skunk. He nearly tripped over his bag trying to pick it up, and then stumbled as he climbed the ladder into the cab of the vehicle. Sitting in the driver's seat, he flipped the lights on. "Have you memorized the information on that piece of paper?"

"I think so."

"Good." He grabbed it out of my hand, pulled a lighter from his pocket, and set it on fire. He let it burn all the way to his fingertips before blowing it out and crumbling the unburned piece of paper up and putting it in his jacket pocket.

"What now?" I asked.

He looked me over for a few long seconds before he finally spoke. "If fate frowns on me in the same way you are, I'd guess I'll be dead pretty soon."

I sighed deeply. "I've woken up to a damn nightmare. A nightmare you helped create. And the look I'm giving you is your goddamn takeaway?"

"I'm acutely aware of what I've done." He paused for a moment, trying to grasp and claw at whatever composure he could muster before continuing. "My daughters, remember? If they're dead, it's because of..." He stopped, his lips quivering. For whatever reason, though, he fought his way through it and finished: "It's because of me."

I wanted to punch the drunk bastard in the face, but I didn't. Maybe his ruminating over the potential demise of his daughters kept me from it. They were sweet girls and didn't deserve any of what was happening.

Having quickly regained his composure, not to mention an unabashed and unrepentant supply of arrogance, he said, "None of this was ever my intention. I'm just a man who got caught up in things that were already in motion—a small cog in the machine that the world has been creating in order to bring us down a notch or two for a long time."

I fought hard to stifle a laugh. "You're so full of shit—"

"Hate me or not, I'm leaving. I'm breaking every rule I have by giving you the information I gave you. No one else can know. Don't let me down."

Don't let me down. I shook my head.

"If I were you, I would go back the way we came before I open this door. This garage is soundproof, but it won't be as soon as I open the door. Good luck, William."

I turned around to leave without saying a word.

Over the whine of the powerful engine, he said, "Remember when I told you I left one of them alive?"

I nodded.

"He's in the second-floor conference room. He'll have answers, but you have to hurry. It's only a matter of time before those people regroup and come back. They'll not make the same mistake of only sending a handful of people this time."

A very small part of me thought about telling him about the large group of Grays that had gathered outside. I didn't. I doubted he would have any issues with them considering the vehicle he was in looked like a tank. Another reason was, I didn't care, really. He deserved whatever fate that befell him. I was sure he would live, though. Cockroaches seemed to be able to live through almost anything.

I didn't bother looking back. I exited through the small passage as the large garage door opened. Once back in Miley's office, I rifled through the backpack he'd given me. There was a wad of cash; hundred-dollar bills, and a lot of them. There was a radio and phone, and just like he'd said, they both worked, aside from the cell phone not having a signal. There was also a GPS receiver, a notebook with some numbers in it, and a few other miscellaneous items, including a key to what I imagined was the other tracked vehicle. A small penitence for all the shit he had caused.

I threw everything back into the bag and hid it under his desk. I then went back to the conference room where everyone was sitting quietly around the long, black-lacquered table. It looked like they were eating MREs. I hadn't seen those since I was a little kid. My uncle would bring home some for me after his summer national guard training. Avery and I would sit around on warm summer days, imagining we were in the army. Avery hadn't liked to play war much. He was more of a strategic planner. That had left me with the dirty work of doing all the fighting. Kind of like real life, honestly.

"The Salisbury steak is pretty good, son. You should try it," Sam said.

"They are better than the ones we used to eat when we were kids," Avery said, smacking his lips.

"Not really in the mood to eat," I said.

Sam's eyes got big. "You not hungry? Must be a pocolypse or somethin."

"Not now, Sam."

He sucked on his fork for a second before saying, "Just tryin ta lighten thangs up is all."

"Will Miley be joining us, soon?" Tish asked.

"No."

Her eyes narrowed. "Why?"

"He left to go find his daughters—"

"So, he's gone?" Tish asked.

Before I could reply, Kelley practically jumped out of her seat. She grabbed her stomach and quickly asked Tish if she would mind watching the baby while she went to the bathroom. Tish flashed a look at the woman. I couldn't tell if it was out of anger or disbelief, or maybe both. She angrily tossed her fork on the table before taking the baby.

"What's that all about?" I asked.

The baby squirmed in Tish's loose embrace. For a moment, I wondered if she was going to let the baby squirm out of her arms. But as if someone had flipped a switch, Tish's demeanor instantly changed. She began to examine the child. "The bitch," she uttered just loudly enough those nearby could hear.

"There's something the matter with this poor baby. She's sick. Not only that. She is white, but Kelley is Inupiat."

"Oh, shit, son. Playin the race card durin end times? Not cool," Sam said, smiling.

"Shut the fuck up," Tish said. I'd never known her to flash so much anger, especially towards Sam.

"Come on, guys," I said.

Tish had the blankets off the baby. "Poor baby girl." She began examining her in earnest. "She's bruised all over her back and bottom."

"Shhh," Titouan said. "Do you hear that? She's whispering to herself."

"Or to someone else," Avery observed.

I ran to the bathroom door and jiggled the knob. I heard the metallic racking of a pistol slide. I cursed silently to myself. How could I have been so stupid? All the signs were there, but I'd completely ignored them. I quickly withdrew my hand from the doorknob. No sooner than I had, the door burst open, and Kelley was through. I caught a quick elbow to my face, causing me to stumble long enough for Kelley to maneuver behind me for cover. Goddamn, she was fast.

"If you move another inch, I'll blow your fucking head off," Kelley said, aiming her pistol at Sam, who had moved way too slowly, due to his injury, towards the rifle leaning against the wall.

"Where are they?" Kelley asked, hot breath and spittle bathed the back of my neck.

"What are you talking about?" I said, my voice was almost embarrassing high pitched.

"Don't play stupid! Miley… and the prisoner he's holding." She waved her pistol to an empty chair at the table. "Have a fucking seat."

"Okay, shit." How would she know who Miley was. And more disturbing, how in the hell did she know about the guy he captured?

Being that it looked like she was my new enemy, and even though Miley was majorly on my shit list, I was going to help him escape. An enemy of my enemy was my friend, came to mind. "Look, I don't know what you're talking about."

"Yes, you do. When my people attacked, he took one of them prisoner. He murdered the rest."

Perplexed, Titouan asked, "Your people?"

Through gritted teeth and a clenched jaw, she said, "My people. That's all you need to know."

"Now, where are they?" She demanded.

"Miley left. I already told you that."

"Where? I'm going to shoot one of them the next time you don't answer my question."

"William, what the hell is going on here?" Titouan asked.

She fired over Titouan's head, missing on purpose.

Looking at Titouan, I said, "Just be quiet. I know where Miley is going, and I know where the guy he captured is, too." Everyone's attention turned to me.

Sam looked confused. "What's goin on, son?"

"You're wasting time. Now tell me!" Kelley yelled.

I motioned for everyone to calm down. "Miley is headed to Prudhoe Bay, and then Fairbanks." I honestly didn't want to tell her exactly where he was going, but there were no clear alternatives. In other words, I couldn't think of a good enough lie she'd believe, so I told her the truth. Miley had a decent head start. That was the best I could do for the bastard.

"And?"

"The person you're looking for is on the second floor, tied up in a conference room," I said.

"If you lie to me, I'm going to make their deaths painful instead of quick," she said, as she frantically typed something out on the phone, having a difficult time because of the pistol she held.

"What about the baby? What the hell have you done to her?" Tish said, her voice trailing off to a whisper.

Kelley seemed genuinely surprised by Tish's sudden outburst. She cocked her head to the side, and, with what bordered on a grin, said, "I poisoned her. Like her parents, she's going to die, but then so are a lot of people."

"You're a bitch," Tish yelled!

Kelley began to say something to Tish but paused. With her smirk from before gone and replaced with an anger-soaked expression, she said, "Watch yourself."

Tish seethed. Her jaw was set hard. I thought she was going to scream or even charge Kelley. Instead, she took a deep breath and closed her eyes. Sam said something to her, but it went unanswered.

Kelley, satisfied that Tish was no longer a problem, nudged me over to where the lone rifle was leaned against the wall. She put the pistol in her waistband and rifle in her hands in one quick, fluid motion. She checked to make sure a round was chambered before saying, "Let's go to that conference room. Now!"

***

I tried to close the door that blocked off the second floor from the third, but Kelley wouldn't let me. She told me that her people would need the door left open, so they could get in. Kelley paused. The second floor was almost completely dark. "Turn on the lamp," she said.

I fumbled with it for a second before finding the switch.

"Hold the lamp up, so I can see where you're taking me," she said, pushing the barrel harder into my back.

"Okay, okay."

Other than making sure Kelley didn't reunite with Miley's prisoner, I didn't have much of a plan. The only thing I had going for me was the pistol Miley had given me hidden in my waistband. I just needed a chance to get to it. I thought about dropping the lamp and going for it, but I'd already seen how nimble and fast Kelley was. I didn't have a chance in hell. I would take her on as long of a wild goose chase as Miley's office building would allow for and hope the opportunity would present itself.

Something occurred to me. There was a small cafeteria in the back of the second floor. Miley had a private dining room where he ate with executives. For reasons only known to Miley, he had the floor lowered in that room. There was a decent step down that if Kelley wasn't prepared for might trip her up enough to give me the time I needed to go for the pistol. I mean, that's all I could come up with. Saving my friends rested on that winner.

Shit. I went for it and failed miserably.

"Well?" She asked, pushing the already embedded barrel deeper into my back.

The cafeteria was no more. It had been completely torn out and was in the midst of a full remodel. "I haven't been down here for a while. They've remodeled the place since I was last here. We'll just have to keep looking..."

"You're stalling."

"It's dark... they've changed things."

"I warned you. Put the lamp down on the floor," she said.

"Come on. I can take you..."

"Now!"

I kneeled enough to sit the lamp down. Sweat poured down my face as I was reacquainted with the rifle barrel. I was afraid and embarrassed. Mostly, though, I was angry with myself. I was a buffoon. I had failed my friends once again. I was going to die without even going for the pistol Miley had given me. Was that what I was going to do. Just die without a fight, I wondered to myself in those last seconds. Did I really lack that much of a spine? "Fuck that," I said aloud, as I went for the pistol in my rear waistband.

Kelley screamed something. Then there was a single loud pop. I recoiled as I felt intense heat on my face. It hurt but not as much as I thought it would. Over the terrible ringing in my ear, Sam yelled something. I heard something else, too. Kelly was chambering another round in the rifle. She had missed everyone on the first try, including me. She must have fired wildly at Sam and Titouan. There was no other reason I was alive.

There was a struggle—a body hit the floor. I fought with the pistol tangled in my belt and oversized fleece top I was wearing. "Goddammit," I yelled.

I saw Kelley swing the butt of the rifle around, catching Titouan hard on his upper shoulder or the side of his face; it was hard to tell. With lightning-quick reflexes, she had her pistol up and ready to fire at Sam, who must've been unlucky enough to be hit with the rifle as well, as he still seemed to be reeling from something.

I finally managed to untangle the pistol and brought it up to firing position just as she was getting ready to shoot Sam. I remember hoping that I'd clicked the safety off before leveling it to fire. Kelley shrieked while staggering backward before finally falling hard to the floor. She lay there screaming and kicking, as much out of anger as anything, I thought.

I kicked the rifle out of her reach, and then picked up the phone she'd dropped. It was big for a modern phone, somewhere between the size and look of a satellite phone and an older Blackberry. On the keys were symbols I didn't recognize—maybe Korean or Chinese. Goosebumps spread up and down my arms as the implications washed over me.

"What do we do with the bitch?" Sam asked, his face set in a hard grimace as he hobbled to my side. With his leg banged up like it was, he was very lucky he didn't end up dead.

"We take her back upstairs. We'll deal with her there." I then handed Sam Kelley's pistol and told Titouan to get the rifle. He didn't move, though. He was probing his mouth with his fingers.

"Are you okay, Titouan?" I asked.

"No!" He walked over to where she sat, and, without any warning, kicked her in the face with his heavy boot. Her neck snapped back with such force, I thought he might've broken it. "You crazy bitch," he spat. Something solid hit the floor.

Kelley was a tough chick. I had to give her that. She angrily pawed at a tear that threatened to run down her cheek, erasing any signs of weakness. With the copious amount of blood flowing from her busted lip and potentially-broken nose, she looked to be possessed. She glowered at Titouan, and he returned the favor, moving ever so slightly back in her direction.

"Easy, son, she'll get hers," Sam said.

"Fuck!" Titouan yelled.

Sam and I gathered her up and took her back upstairs.

When we got back to the conference room, Avery stood at the door, nervously awaiting our fate, while Tish sat in the corner of the room, blankly staring at what seemed like nothing. From what I could tell, the baby was no longer with us. She lay limp in Tish's equally limp embrace.

Tish finally looked up as I sat Kelley down hard in one of the executive chairs. The two of them exchanged angry glances, but no words were proffered. Kelley didn't flinch or look away. There was no remorse or anything bordering guilt residing on her anger-ladened and battered face.

I asked Avery to fetch me some duct tape and a wet rag. He quickly did as I bade.

"You alright, bud?" He didn't answer. Instead, he gave me what I asked for before walking over to where the baby's blankets were, grabbed them, and draped them over both Tish and baby.

I turned my attention back to Kelley. She's lucky as hell I was a terrible shot. The bullet had grazed the side of her shoulder pretty good, but not enough where she would bleed out. With a few stitches, she'd be fine. As for her nose, it was broken. I let her wipe the blood from her face while I applied the bandage.

"Go get the bastard from the conference room. Make sure you lock the stairwell doors on your way back up. They'll be coming sooner than later," I said.

Sam checked the pistol for ammunition and headed out the door. Titouan slung the rifle over his shoulder and was on Sam's heels.

"Titouan," I said, "he needs to be alive. No stupid shit."

He spat another mouthful of blood but nodded his head in agreement.

After she was cleaned up and bandaged, I secured her to the chair with the duct tape. Only then did I check her pockets for weapons or other useful things. I suppose I should've done that before taping her up like a mummy, but frisking was new to me. She spat a bloody glob on me as I removed a small vial of white powder from a small pocket on the front of her coat. The poison, I thought.

I wiped the spit off my face without bothering to say a word. I didn't want to give her the satisfaction.

"I found this hidden in the baby blankets," Avery said.

Tish asked to see it, but she was interrupted by Kelley's expletives towards Avery. I told Kelley I would tape her damn mouth up if she didn't shut up. She slammed her head into the headrest of the chair, cursed, and settled into a hard stare at me.

Avery rebuffed Tish in favor of giving what he'd found to me. It looked like a small tube of toothpaste. You wouldn't have wanted to brush your teeth with it, though. Whatever the stuff in the tube was, a little of it went a long way, and damn did it smell terrible. I then realized the stuff on Kelley's coat smelled exactly like the stuff in the tube—exactly like the Grays.

"They're the same, aren't they, William?" Avery asked.

Before I could answer, the conference room door opened. Sam and Titouan dragged a man inside. He looked to be about as bloody and battered as I was. I remembered the bruising on Miley's hands. I wondered what answers he had that he didn't bother telling me. I would get my own answers. I hoped I wouldn't have to resort to violence as Miley had.

I pulled a chair over to where the man was roughly made to sit. Like I had with Kelley, I gave him a good wrapping of duct tape. Enough to make him uncomfortable and hold him firmly in place. I spun him around in a direction where I could talk to both he and Kelley at the same time.

As the man became more in-tune with his surroundings, he finally chanced a look over at Kelley, who had been sitting next to him the entire time. He seemed to have prepared himself for the worst. He was putting on his best nothing-gets-to-me attitude, but that carefully-crafted persona fell apart, even if for just an instant when his eyes locked on to Kelley's. She croaked something that resembled his name before falling completely silent.

The whole exchange lasted only a few seconds, but it was just long enough that I knew the two were more than colleagues in some evil organization. They shared something deeper. Even though that gave me an advantage in our negotiation or interrogation, or whatever the hell it was, I soon found out neither of them was much for telling me the things I needed to know. Not without the proper motivation anyway.

"What's your name?" I asked the man.

"Bob," he said, surprisingly affable for someone who'd been beaten to a pulp. From the bloody bandage on his thigh, it was clear he had also been shot.

"Well, Bob, we need some answers, and you're going to give them to us."

"I don't know anything, but I wouldn't tell you if I did," he said, smiling like he was posing for a picture.

"That could lead to some bad things for you and Kelley, but I would prefer it not to come to that."

"You'll do what you need to do, of course," he said, grimacing, as he moved his injured leg.

Kelley seemed pleased by this. "We aren't going to talk, you monster."

Tish, by this point, was standing uncomfortably close to Kelley and Bob and pacing back and forth. Her face was painted in a scowl, and her hands shook as she walked. I looked at Sam. He just shook his head and gave a worried shrug.

"There's a comfortable couch in Miley's office if you need to rest," I told her.

"I'm fine," she replied. She wasn't.

I turned most of my attention back to the interrogation. "So, Bob, what are you doing in Barrow?"

"I'm a cab driver. You wouldn't believe the money you can make up here. I've been sending money home to my folks back in Boston. In ten years, I'll have made more than most people make in two times that," he said. I wasn't buying any of it. I'd seen Avery show more enthusiasm talking about electromagnetism.

"Boston, huh? You don't have much of a Boston accent," I said.

Bob cocked his head and grinned. "Been gone for a while."

Titouan's face was blood red, Sam wasn't overly enthused, and Tish was wearing a groove in the floor. I was losing control of the entire situation. I needed to get them to talk, or I was going to have a revolt.

"How long are we going to sit here and wait for them to talk? They know something," Titouan said, favoring his jaw.

"That's why we're talking, to get answers."

His lips turned to thin ribbons as anger beseeched him. "They aren't going to talk. We have to make them."

I was about to tell him to calm down, but before I could, he flung a heavy stapler at Bob. It hit him on the left side of the face, causing a large laceration below the cheekbone and extending to his earlobe. At least the fucker's smile was gone. It was replaced with a loathing I'd never seen up until that point in my life. If he'd had the chance, he would've killed Titouan with his own bare hands.

"Dammit. We're not doing that, Titouan," I said. "Get your shit straight, or you're going to have to leave the room."

I saw Sam shaking his head out of the corner of my eye. "Titouan's right, son. Look at 'at sonofabitch. He'd kill us in a second if he thanks he can. You know what? Fuck 'em, William. 'Ey want ta play like 'is, we might hafta play 'at way, too."

Never looking away from the phone, Avery asked, "Why do we need them to talk, at all?"

"What?" I asked.

"We have this." Avery picked up Kelley's phone and held it aloft for everyone to see.

Bob shot Kelley an evil glare. Another tell.

"If I can crack this phone, I should be able to glean a considerable amount of information about who these people are and what they have done. The hard part will be learning Korean, but with enough time, I believe it can be done."

"So North-damn-Korea, then?" Sam asked.

Avery thought for a moment before answering. "That is a decent supposition considering our shared history."

Silence filled the room. I wanted what Avery said to percolate with Bob and Kelley a little while before continuing with the quasi-interrogation. While I was fairly sure Avery would crack the phone, there was no way to be certain. Bob and Kelley didn't need to know that, though. I wanted them to think it was a forgone conclusion that he could. Besides, it would be a lot quicker if they would just tell us what was going on.

The dead air was too much for Bob. I could see he was close to breaking, so I kept waiting. After maybe five minutes of silence, his guard was lifted, if only briefly. Not what I was hoping for, but it showed he could break under the right circumstances.

"Now, they'll know..." He stopped himself, and after regaining a modicum of control, he continued with the lines we would become accustomed to from the Order. "You were supposed to have killed the phone. You brought dishonor to you, your family, the Order, and most significantly, our great leader."

Avery uttered something under his breath, maybe a prayer, and after a couple seconds, he said, "I have it booted up. The phone's software is based on Linux Kernel. I can work with that in my sleep. If I can get into the phone, and assuming I can learn even cursory Korean, there should be a great deal of intel on this phone."

"Looks like I don't need you guys. I can find out what's on that phone."

Kelley began to cry. She turned to Bob and said, "I'm sorry."

"Think of the cause, dammit," Bob said.

"When I learned you had been captured, I knew I had to do something." Kelley, realizing she was saying too much, broke into Korean for the rest of what she said.

"You know it doesn't work that way. We're both dead now." He then said something quickly in Korean.

Kelley shook off whatever Bob had said, and then turned towards Avery. "You should leave the phone alone. It doesn't ask for an access code, and you must know how to enter it. It will wipe itself if they try to access any of the messages."

The phone became like a hot potato in his hands. He quickly sat the phone down on the table.

"Okay. Why would you—" I began before being interrupted.

"William, you can't listen to her. If she gives you a code, it won't be what you think it'll be! Don't listen to her!" Tish yelled.

"Let 'is play out, girl," Sam said, putting his hands up in a placating manner.

"More like let them play us," she scowled.

"Just stop," I told her.

"Why would you tell them that?"

"Because she wants to live, Bob. Why don't you help her."

"None of us will have any choice in the matter when this place is stormed, and they kill every single one of us. Kelley and I are disposable, especially so, now," Bob said, tears and blood streaming down his face.

"We're not disposable, and your friends aren't here yet. How about you talk, and we let you go before they get here. We'll worry about ourselves."

"What happens when they run back to their people and tell them we're here with this damn phone, William? They can't live," Titouan said.

Bob, going through a wide range of emotions, broke into a string of angry Korean aimed at Titouan.

"You and Tish are losing your shit. I need you guys to calm the fuck down."

Sam joined in the chorus. "I swear to God, son, if you speak in 'at shit one more time, I'm goin ta walk over 'ere and cut yer little piener off, ya sonofabitch. William is a might bit nicer 'an I am.... Too damn nice."

Bob sniffled but managed to battle back from his momentary lapse in composure. "You're losing your friends. They'll turn on you long before this place is overtaken.... long before you get anything from us."

"My friends are like family. We might disagree about things, but we'll hang together. Tell us what you know, and we'll all make it out of this."

"I don't think so—" Bob said.

"What can you offer us?" Kelley interrupted, choosing to take the opposite tact of Bob.

"You can't, Kelley—"

I told Bob I'd tape his damn mouth shut if he didn't close it.

Kelley's eyes flitted as she looked at Bob. Her face didn't bear any resemblance to the one I'd come to know. There was a genuine, if fleeting, tenderness to her expressions. She was torn, there was no doubt about that, but it was clear there was something in her life more important than the stupid Order, or whatever the hell it was called.

For Bob's part, he struggled with the signals she was sending. It was clear by watching him that he cared about her, even though he managed to stay much more guarded than she had. That was until he finally found out what her weakness was. What his weakness would be.

She shook her head in the affirmative to Bob, gave Sam a quick probing glance, and began to say something to Bob in Korean. Bob's face metamorphosed into something he fought hard to stop but had no power against. Whatever it was she'd told him, it had a profound effect on him. He was now just an early twenty-something male. The pretext that existed just moments ago was, at least for the time being, something that was suddenly much less important. I had them.

I focused on Kelley. She was the weak link. "Talk, Kelley."

"Dammit, William. You can't listen to her. She killed a baby for God's sake. Do you really think she's going to tell you the truth," she said. Tish was just less than an arm's length away from Kelley at that point. I thought she might attack her, or worse.

"Sam," I said. Knowing without my telling him, Sam limped towards Tish.

"I think it's time for you guys to get our things ready to leave. I'll handle the rest of this." I looked at Sam, specifically. "I got this."

He examined me for an uncomfortably long time before finally complying. As Sam guided everyone out of the room, I was struck by something. The trust my friends had in me wasn't boundless. By not including them in the decision-making process, I was straining the bond that held us together.

Before Sam left the room, I told him to gather up the supplies that Miley had left for us. I told him that only he and Titouan should have access to the weapons. He left the room without as much as a grunt. Tish, however, was letting her displeasure be known.

She ran back into the room. "Goddamn it, William, don't listen to those animals. They'll trick you, and we'll end up dead."

Tish and Kelley shared odd glances.

"Tish, please. I'll handle this. You have to help the others with the supplies."

"Get off me, Sam!" Tish yelled before jerking free from Sam's grasp. She then stumped down the hallway. Sam shook his head and then followed.

Avery was last out of the room. He nearly walked into a chair because he couldn't take his eyes off the phone. He closed the door behind him. I waited a few moments before I began talking to Bob and Kelley. Once I thought we had our privacy, I didn't waste any time. "If I'm even a percent as good as I think I am at reading people, Kelley is pregnant. Let me help you guys, please."

Kelley began to shake her head in protest but couldn't hold back the torrent of emotions that had crippled her will. And oddly enough, she chose to speak in English, which still puzzles me to this day. Maybe she was trying at that point to garner more of my sympathy. She wanted to live whatever life she, Bob, and Baby could eke out, so by that point, she was doing everything in her power not to anger me. Why Bob chose to follow suit is even more confusing. Whatever the reason, I will never know. "I'm sorry for not telling you, Bob. I knew none of this was supposed to happen—we weren't supposed to happen."

"Do you believe him?" Bob asked Kelley.

"I am a man of my word. I just want my friends to be safe. I know you guys aren't the planners of all this crap. I don't care about you. I just want to live through this, and I know you two do too. So live, dammit. Allow your baby to live."

Bob had one more foray of insults in him for us. "We were taught that you are all liars and cheats. I don't believe a word you say."

"Dammit, Bob, we're running out of time. My friends are all I got right now, and I'll do everything in my power to protect them. If you love Kelley like it seems she loves you, you're responsible for her, and you're certainly responsible for the damn baby she's carrying. Tell me what you fucking know. Now!"

"Our oath, Kelley!" He yelled. He then slumped in his seat, thought for a few seconds, and replied more softly, "I love you... but can't. My oath to our family, country, and to our Dear Leader doesn't allow it." He fought back from the precipice. His back stiffened, before finishing, "I can't."

Kelley looked at me and then at Bob, and then asked, "What do you need me to tell you?"

"Everything."

***

"William!" Someone screamed my name. I was in shock, which wasn't uncommon during those early days, but this time was different. My view of the world was completely upended in the short time it took Kelley to tell me what she knew. It was shattering. Things were never going to be the same. Not in my lifetime, anyway. Maybe never.

"Are you alright?" I felt a light pressure on my shoulder.

Pictures flashed through my mind. Put together, they produced the effect of a flipbook. A great many were of good times I'd had growing up. There were pictures of birthday parties at Avery's, which were always great. The one that kept popping up the most was a picture of mom. She was sad, but she was almost always sad in pictures. I wanted to hug her one last time, but I couldn't. All my anger towards her was gone, dissipated like the heat from the pistol that suddenly felt heavy in my hand.

"You have to get up, William. Please," Titouan said.

I remember holding the pistol. I didn't remember how it got in my hands, though.

"Shit. There're vehicles outside, and hundreds—maybe thousands—of Grays. We gotta go, son," Sam said.

I told them the Grays couldn't get in, and not to worry... I then remembered feeling pain across my face. Somebody slapped me.

"It ain't just damn Grays. There's a bunch of people like those two," someone said.

Like Kelley and Bob, I thought. Yeah. Then I remembered. "No," I whimpered. "I shouldn't have done that..."

I think I was standing at that point. I didn't want to look, but I knew I had to. There was blood everywhere. There was blood on me, and even in my mouth, which was becoming too damn common. The metallic taste made me want to vomit again, but I somehow managed not to.

"Last time! They're on the second floor right now. Get your shit together, or they're going to kill us! We're going to have to fight," I remember Titouan saying.

There was gunfire outside and glass breaking somewhere. I had to get my shit together. I wasn't going to let my friends down again, and I needed to be a man about what I'd done. I needed to see it. It would be closure, of sorts. It was just a snapshot of the coming brutality—the remorseless world we'd woken up to. If I was going to keep my humanity, I needed to own up to my own cruelty. It hurt to see what I'd done... but that meant, I still felt remorse. That separated me from those who intended to harm my friends and me.

Kelley's face was gone. Bob's face was mostly intact. I must have been about out of bullets by the time I got to him. I made one count to the forehead, though. He wasn't going to walk away, that much was sure. They sure as fuck weren't going to live out their goddamn love story with all the pain they had helped cause. I made sure of that. It felt wrong, though, but everything was wrong.

Kelley was pregnant, though... Dammit.

Avery patted me on the shoulder. I remember that as well as what he said. "We have to go, bud."

"Alright," I said.

"We're going to have to fight our way out," Titouan said, in a voice I almost didn't recognize. He was changing. I wasn't sure for the good or not, but he was changing, nonetheless.

"No more fighting. At least for now, anyway." Everyone jumped as a loud noise came from one of the floors below us. "Follow me."

Sam paused, unsure whether to trust my crazy ass. "You better know what you doin or we screwed."

"I'm good. I'm okay," I said.

As the others grabbed as much as they could carry, I remembered the backpack Miley had given me. I reached under the desk and grabbed it. I then opened the large cabinet door that led to the secret stairwell. With another bang sounding from just down the hall, no one had time to linger on the oddity of Miley having a secret passage.

Once in the garage, I handed a flabbergasted Sam the keys to the vehicle. Without comment, he hopped in and started the engine. It fired up on the first try. Everyone else loaded the provisions into the back of the vehicle. Within just a few moments, all of us were loaded in and ready to go. Sam looked at me.

As scared and confused as I was at that moment, I understood the necessity of an expedient exit from the garage. Competing with that necessity was the overwhelming fear I felt after hearing Kelley and Bob's admissions—the fear I knew my friends would feel when I told them about what I'd learned. It was no longer a theorizing game in which I hoped for the best, and the worst was just something that happened in movies or on TV. If the Order was successful, the world outside that garage was going to be a terrible place.

I wanted to savor one last moment in the garage. I then pressed the button on the garage door opener. "Let's go."

Authors Note:

Well, there you have it, my first ever book. One of the first iterations of this book was written in 2014. During which time it was going to be more of an alien-versus-us kind of book. The Patch, William, and Avery were still in that version, but you would hardly recognize them. William was a nerdy scholar type, while Avery was kind of undefined—more of a tertiary character at best. The Patch was still a thing. Actually, the entire story, for me, revolved around the Patch, even though the first book didn't linger there too long. The thought at the time was, I wanted to write something about a cold, dark, and isolated place. Everything else sort of was created off that premise.

You'll notice that some of the Grays act slightly differently than what is assumed from zombies. They carried, and on some level, knew how to use, weapons. Although this isn't exactly new in zombie literature, I wanted that to be the starting point. In other words, I tried to repurpose zombies into weapons. This is where the Order comes into play.

As the story progressed, I started reading about CRISPR editing tools, and this really changed the arc of the story more than anything else. My thinking was, if the average Joe could get his hands on tools that would allow him to edit the human genome, what would happen if an entire country (or countries) put their collective energy into using genome editing for nefarious reasons. Well, they could do some terrible things. Look for more of this in book two.

Hopefully, the story was enjoyable for you. It's been a longtime coming for me to finish these books. I do work full-time at my non-writing gig, so my schedule is tight. Having said that, I do plan on publishing book two in August or September.

Lastly, if you could do one thing for me, I would appreciate it. I need reviews, good or bad. As a new author, that helps me more than anything, both in how the book ranks, but also in my learning curve. I've had friends and family offer to write reviews, and I have forbidden it. For them to be beneficial, they have to be real. So, please, please do that for me. Thank you so very much in advance. It is much appreciated.

Made in United States
Orlando, FL
04 December 2023

40108528R00127